The
FAIREST

ANNE SCHRAFF

SADDLEBACK
EDUCATIONAL PUBLISHING

2/13

PA

URBAN UNDERGROUND

A Boy Called Twister
The Fairest
If You Really Loved Me
Like a Broken Doll
One of Us
Outrunning the Darkness
The Quality of Mercy
Shadows of Guilt
To Be a Man
Wildflower

SADDLEBACK
EDUCATIONAL PUBLISHING
www.sdlback.com

© 2011 by Saddleback Educational Publishing

ISBN-13: 978-1-61651-007-7
ISBN-10: 1-61651-007-2
eBook: 978-1-60291-792-7

Printed in Guangzhou, China
0811/CA21101408

15 14 13 12 11   3 4 5 6

CHAPTER ONE

Alonee Lennox and Sami Archer were walking toward their sociology classroom when they noticed a large cluster of girls at the door.

"Look at that," Sami noted. "Looks like they're givin' somethin' away. I hope it's chocolate chip cookies or maybe cinnamon buns. I ate breakfast this morning but I'm still hungry."

When they reached the door, the girls saw a large, colorful flyer decorated with medieval jesters and streamers.

The Medieval Fair is coming. All junior girls are eligible to be Princess of the Fair. Be sure to vote for the girl you feel best exemplifies the qualities of our namesake— Harriet Tubman.

Alonee recalled, "Oh yeah, I heard about that. It's going to be on a Saturday with food booths and crafts."

"Gonna turn out to be a beauty contest," Sami complained. "All the pretty chicks gonna be clawin' and scratchin' to win. See, Lawson's is giving a bunch of clothes to the winner. Local TV gonna cover the thing. Some cute chick gonna be wantin' to prance and preen for the cameras."

Ms. Gayle Amsterdam, a bubbly twenty-four-year old, was the sociology teacher. Ms. Amsterdam was overflowing with enthusiasm for her subject and her students. Just out of college, she often seemed more like one of the kids than a teacher. Before starting class this morning, she beamed out at the students. Then she announced, "I think it's so exciting that we're choosing a junior girl to preside over our fair. She will be a lovely girl, because *all* our girls are lovely. She'll also be a girl who is friendly and filled with school spirit. She must be a girl everybody would like to know!"

Ryann Kern raised her hand. She was not beautiful but she was pleasant looking. She was from a small town in Alabama. Her only close friend so far at Tubman was Leticia Hicks, from the same Alabama town. "Ms. Amsterdam, do you have to fill out an application to be considered for Princess of the Fair?" she asked.

Marko Lane leaned over to his girlfriend, Jasmine Benson. He whispered, "Like that chick would ever make it!"

"No, no, Ryann," Ms. Amsterdam replied. "That's the beauty of this contest. Every junior girl is automatically a candidate. There are no entry forms. We don't want any campaigning. We want it pure and honest. We want all the juniors—boys and girls—to pick that special girl. She has to be someone who has touched their heart and who will be the perfect Princess of the Fair."

Marko Lane looked over at Jasmine. "You're it, babe. You're the prettiest chick on campus," he told her.

Jasmine smiled back at Marko. She was beautiful and she knew it. Few junior girls came even close to her in that department. And already the wheels were turning in Jasmine's mind. This could be a stepping stone to something better, a really important beauty pageant.

Ms. Amsterdam bubbled on, her pretty, round face wreathed in smiles. Only a few short years ago, she was a high school girl herself, a spirited cheerleader. She had not changed much. She delighted in the social activities at Tubman High. She was reliving her own joyful high school days. The Princess of the Fair contest was her idea. She was its chairperson.

"It'll be a lovely, colorful fair with food and crafts and music," Ms. Amsterdam was saying. "Some worthwhile charities will have booths. There'll be local musicians, dancers, and even a few clowns, for the children."

When Ms. Amsterdam finally got around to her sociology lecture, nobody was paying any attention. Everybody was speculating on who would become the Princess of the Fair. Alonee thought the idea was lame. The fair sounded like fun, but the princess contest would lead to hard feelings, she thought.

After class, Alonee walked to the vending machine with Oliver Randall.

"Well, I know who I'm voting for," Oliver told her, as he picked a bright red apple from the machine.

"It's a silly idea," Alonee commented. She pulled out an orange and started peeling it. "Ms. Amsterdam said the girl who wins needs to have good qualities like Harriet Tubman had. But you know what'll happen, don't you? It's going to be all about beauty. Like those stupid Miss Whatever contests on TV. The girls all parade around in skimpy bathing suits and pretty gowns. Every one of them is stunning. Then they say drippy things about how much they care about animals or homeless people. As if that makes any difference in who wins. A girl could win the Nobel Peace Prize. But if she wasn't gorgeous, she'd never be Miss America, or Miss Universe, or Miss Anything."

"Yeah, you're right," Oliver agreed. "But I still think you'd make a cute princess."

Alonee gave Oliver a playful shove. "Like I'd win," she laughed. "It's going to go to some girl who is absolutely beautiful, in a striking way. Like Sereeta." Sereeta Prince was now dating Jaris Spain, the boy Alonee had secretly loved for a long while. At one time, Alonee had had a fantasy that she and Jaris would eventually get together. But now she was falling in love with Oliver. She didn't think of Jaris anymore in that way.

Sereeta had honey-colored skin and masses of black curls. She had large, expressive eyes and sweeping lashes. Alonee liked Sereeta. They had been friends since childhood. Sereeta was a good person too. Alonee thought Sereeta had what it takes to be Princess of the Fair as well as anybody.

As Alonee and Oliver were leaving the vending machine, Marko and Jasmine came along.

"Dude," Marko called, "this chick here on my arm, she's the Princess of the Fair. Right here. Jasmine is eye candy. Y'hear what I'm saying? Is this a doll or what?"

Oliver smiled. "Jasmine's a pretty girl, yeah," he agreed. "But like Ms. Amsterdam said, all the junior girls are lovely. The princess has to have a heart of gold too, right?" Oliver had not been at Tubman High for long. But he already knew Jasmine's reputation as a mean girl.

"Jasmine, she's got that too," Marko declared. "There's nothin' she wouldn't do for me. This is one generous babe." Marko put his arm around Jasmine's shoulders. "Am I right, baby? Don't you take good care of your guy?"

Jasmine didn't smile. She spoke out loud but to herself. "The princess has to be somebody who's a do-gooder for other people, not just her boyfriend." Jasmine didn't get involved in any charity projects. She didn't collect food for Thanksgiving baskets or put together packages for the needy or for the troops serving overseas. Now she was worried that this might hurt her chances of becoming the Princess of the Fair.

"Alonee," Jasmine asked, "you know that group you belong to? The one where you take these foster kids around to the movies and camping and stuff? That thing Pastor Bromley put together. Maybe I could get into that. You still need teenagers to mentor with the little losers you buddy up with?"

Alonee looked at Oliver who covered his mouth with his hand to hide his smile. Then Alonee replied, "We don't call them 'little losers,' Jasmine. They're kids from foster homes. They ended up under the care of the county through no fault of their own. Their parents made mistakes, not the kids."

"Whatever," Jasmine grumped impatiently. "You got any openings that I could still get in on?"

"Not right now, Jasmine," Alonee responded. "All the children in the program have assigned teen mentors. We needed mentors back when Destini Fletcher signed on. Remember you made fun of the project, Jasmine? You said camping in the dusty old woods with a bunch of juvenile delinquents was stupid. You asked Destini if she was wigged out or something to be doing that."

Jasmine frowned, an angry look on her face. "She tell you that?" Jasmine snarled, "She's a dirty little backbiter talking about me like that. She ain't never gonna be Princess of the Fair. She's plain as an old whitewashed fence." Jasmine stalked away with Marko in tow.

Alonee heard Jasmine saying to Marko as they left, "I gotta find something to do that makes me look good, Marko. What did Amsterdam say? Girl has to be friendly and filled with school spirit? She's gotta be like old Harriet Tubman in doing good stuff for others. You hear what I'm sayin', Marko? It's not enough that I'm beautiful."

"Yeah," Marko agreed, "but I wouldn't worry too much, babe. Nobody's going to pay much attention to all that stuff the teacher was saying. Like they don't pay no attention to what the preachers say. They'll do what they wanna do. And that's pick the most gorgeous babe in the school. That's you, Jasmine. Especially when the guys vote, they're gonna to be voting for the hottest babe, and you smokin', Jaz."

Marko and Jasmine disappeared around a corner. Alonee shook her head. "What makes me think this contest is a really, *really* bad idea, Oliver?"

Oliver was laughing. "Maybe because some of the girls are starting to sound a bit like Cinderella's evil stepsisters," he chuckled.

"I know Ms. Amsterdam had good intentions in coming up with this," Alonee remarked. "And she's really a nice person and she's a good teacher too. She knows her stuff. But I think maybe she didn't get enough of the rah-rah-shish-boom-bah when she was a teen. Maybe she's kind of carrying it into Tubman High."

Sami Archer heard what Alonee said. She laughed out loud. "Nice thing about contests like this, I don't gotta worry about beatin' anybody out. Nobody gonna see Sami Archer as no Princess of the Fair. For one thing, there's too much of Sami Archer. My daddy says big like me is beautiful. And I gotta believe my daddy 'cause he's the best. But my size ain't hot around here. Suckas around here go for the skinny Minnies. Tell you one thing, though. If Jasmine Benson gets to be Princess of the Fair, Harriet Tubman's spirit gonna come back to life and give the girl a good thrashin'."

Alonee and Oliver had lunch under the eucalyptus trees with Jaris and Sereeta. Sereeta was wearing a top with red stripes. She looked even more striking than usual. She was very slender, and now Alone thought she looked as if she had lost even more weight. As Sereeta opened her cup of low-fat yogurt, Alonee asked, "Everything okay with you, Sereeta?'

"Oh yeah," Sereeta replied. "Grandma wasn't feeling too good this morning. They got her on this new blood pressure medicine and it's making her groggy. But she'll be okay." In middle school, Sereeta had gone through a lot of pain when her parents divorced. Then they both remarried and got involved in their new lives. Now they both had sort of forgotten about Sereeta. She was a leftover from a less than happy time in their lives. They preferred to ignore her. Luckily, Sereeta was happily settled in with her grandmother.

"What do you think of the Princess of the Fair contest, Sereeta?" Alonee asked.

"I hate it," Sereeta replied. "It's stupid."

"Lot of guys are going to vote for you, Sereeta," Jaris said.

"Isn't there a way out of it?" Sereeta protested. "The last thing in the world I need is that stupid stuff. They wouldn't be voting for me because they like me. It's all a skin-deep thing. They don't even know me. I can't imagine what Ms. Amsterdam was thinking."

"Ms. Amsterdam is like a kid herself," Alonee commented. "She's still got that high school enthusiasm. The principal and vice principal must have approved it. Maybe they think it'll raise school spirit or something."

"Well," Sereeta said, "it's not even just beauty. It's popularity too. I'm not popular and I'm glad. A lot of kids think I'm weird because . . . well, because I guess I am."

"No, you're not," Jaris said loyally.

Sereeta smiled at Jaris and patted his hand. She told him, "You'd say that if I dyed my hair green and swung into school on a vine. The truth is I'm depressed half the time. That's no fun. Things have been so messed up in my house that I'm bawling most of the time. What's that quote? 'Laugh and the world laughs with you, cry and you cry alone.' I don't want to win and

13

I won't. If by cruel fate I did win, I'd have a nervous breakdown."

"Well, Sereeta," Oliver told her, "you could always abdicate. Royal people can do that. If you're a princess, you can hurl the tiara back at them and step down."

Sereeta gave Oliver a big smile. "I like that, Oliver," Sereeta chuckled. "That's a wonderful idea. It won't happen. But if I do win, I'll turn it down. 'Thank you so much for this ridiculous title, which I don't deserve. But I cannot wear this tiara because I am unworthy.' "

Sereeta had to leave the lunch group early. She had to discuss a project with Ms. McDowell, the American history teacher. Jaris, Oliver, and Alonee remained under the eucalyptus trees a little longer.

"Is she okay, Jaris?" Alonee asked.

Jaris nodded slowly. "I think so," he answered. "She's awfully fragile. Her mother has these spells when she wants Sereeta to come home. Sereeta's stepfather doesn't want her home. But, you know, her mom feels guilty. She'll call Sereeta and say, 'Don't you love your mommy anymore?' and Sereeta cries. Finally Sereeta's in a good place where she feels safe. I just hope they leave her alone."

"It must be hard to have that much stress, especially for a sixteen-year-old girl," Oliver remarked. "I mean, we have enough of a struggle figuring out where we fit in this world without that stuff."

When Alonee and Oliver walked back toward their afternoon classes, Alonee told Oliver about Sereeta's struggles. "She cried all during middle school when her parents split. Her dad remarried and moved far away. Her mom got remarried and they have a new baby. Sereeta doesn't get along with her stepfather. A while ago he talked her mother into sending her away to boarding school for her senior year, away from all her friends. Luckily her grandma came to the rescue. So Sereeta's okay now."

"You can see the pain in the girl's eyes," Oliver noted. "She has such pretty eyes. But the pain is there."

Alonee and Oliver went into Mr. Pippin's English class. He wasn't there yet. He usually arrived as late as he could because he had grown to hate teaching. His rowdy students had worn him down. He was just looking forward to retiring in a few years.

Suddenly, Ms. Amsterdam, her arms filled with flyers about the Princess of the Fair contest, appeared in the doorway. She looked like a high school girl with her bright clothing and her wild, curly hair. "Hi, you guys," she gushed to the students already seated. "I don't think Mr. Pippin would mind if I put up some of these flyers on the bulletin board. I want everybody to know about the fair and the contest."

"Well . . ." Oliver said in a cautious voice. He feared Mr. Pippin *would* mind.

Ms. Amsterdam was pinning her flyers to the board as Mr. Pippin came in, lugging his battered briefcase. "What? What are you doing?" he demanded.

"Oh, Mr. Pippin, I was just putting up a few flyers for the Princess of the Fair contest. You know we're choosing a junior girl—" Ms. Amsterdam responded cheerfully.

"Please, Ms. Amsterdam," Mr. Pippin insisted, "I have enough trouble without bringing that nonsense in here."

"Oh, I'm sorry," Ms. Amsterdam sputtered. "I just thought—"

"I don't need a cartoon flyer depicting clowns and balloons on my board," Mr. Pippin stormed. Ms. Amsterdam looked hurt. She seemed almost in tears. Alonee thought she was a little immature. The other day when one of her students said a test was unfair, Ms. Amsterdam got teary eyed. Alonee had never seen a teacher almost cry in class. "My classroom is enough of a circus as it is," Mr. Pippin ranted on. "Please, take your flyers away. I don't want the students talking about that idiotic—"

"Mr. Pippin," Ms. Amsterdam interrupted in an aggrieved voice, "it is not idiotic. It's a wonderful, lovely project to encourage school spirit here at Tubman. I thought you would be interested in promoting that. But if you're not I will just take my flyers down."

"Yes, do that, Ms. Amsterdam," Mr. Pippin said. "The last thing I need in this classroom is a clown poster."

Ms. Amsterdam was sniffling as she pulled the pushpins out of the corkboard. One flyer flew from her hands and fluttered to the floor.

"Good grief," Mr. Pippin groaned as the flyer went under his desk.

Alonee glanced at Oliver. He was having a hard time keeping a straight face. Oliver jumped from his chair, retrieved the flyer, and handed it to Ms. Amsterdam. She thanked him. Then she hurried from the classroom, clutching her flyers like a frightened child.

Mr. Pippin sat down at his desk and briefly pressed his fingers into his closed eyes. His sighs were so loud that they sounded like rushing wind on a stormy day. As the students came filing in, he stared at them. Distaste contorted his face. There was Marko, smirking. Then came Jasmine, giggling. Two boys elbowed each other on their way to their desks. Mr. Pippin's eyes narrowed and his mouth grew small and tight.

"Hi, Mr. Pippin," Marko said. "My girl— Jasmine. She's so hot she's gonna be a shoo-in for Princess of the Fair." Marko swung into his desk. He scraped it along the floor a few inches and made a loud shrieking sound.

CHAPTER TWO

The following day, Thursday, Ryann Kern came to school looking totally different than she had ever looked. Her hair was reddish where it had been dark. It had been shorter. Now it was long with beautiful curls. She had been to the hair salon and gotten extensions. You couldn't tell where her real hair ended and the extensions began. Her eyebrows had been plucked and shaped. She wore hot pink lipstick.

"What do you think, Leticia?" Ryann asked her best and only friend. Leticia Hicks was very plain. She accepted the fact that no amount of styling could change her appearance. "You look amazing, Ryann," she gushed. In recent weeks the girls had

had a falling out over Ryann's interest in boys. Now they were close again.

"Leticia, I so want to be the Princess of the Fair," Ryann admitted. "Imagine getting those cool clothes at Lawson's. Wow—when you're Princess of the Fair, the guys are gonna notice you!"

Leticia looked a little sad. Lately all Ryann seemed to think about was boys. Leticia feared that if Ryann ever got a steady boyfriend, she would ignore Leticia. Leticia was dreading the day when her only friend would vanish from her life.

Derrick Shaw was walking by with his girlfriend, Destini Fletcher. Ryann thought Destini was pretty, but not beautiful. She wasn't Ryann's real competition for the title of Princess of the Fair. The serious competition came from stunning girls like Sereeta Prince and Jasmine Benson.

"Hi," Ryann greeted the pair. "What do you think of the new Ryann Kern?"

Derrick looked puzzled. "You look a lot different. I didn't even recognize you at first. How did your hair get so long?" he asked.

"I got my hair done!" Ryann snapped. "Are you so dumb you never heard of that?"

Destini started to laugh. "Ryann, you're like . . . weird looking," she chuckled.

"What are you saying?" Ryann cried. "I went to a hair salon and a cosmetics counter. They all said I looked great now. Are you jealous or something?"

"You looked nice before, Ryann," Destini told her. "Why are you doing all this?"

"For the contest. To be Princess of the Fair," Ryann replied. "Don't you want to win the contest, Destini?"

Destini laughed again. "I'd never win the contest. I'm not pretty enough. The girl who wins will be really awesome. I'm not even a six on a scale of one to ten."

"You're ten to me, Destini," Derrick chimed in. "I like you just fine."

"Girls like us don't stand a chance, Ryann," Destini said. Leticia looked like she wanted to say something too but she didn't.

"What do you mean 'girls like us'?" Ryann snapped. "Speak for yourself, girl. The lady at the cosmetics counter said I had wonderful high cheekbones. All I needed was a little makeup to look fabulous."

"She was just trying to sell you her expensive junk," Destini remarked. "They charge tons of money for some oily goop that's supposed to make you beautiful. But it doesn't work."

Marko Lane came walking down the path and looked at Ryann. "What are you supposed to be—a clown?" he asked.

Ryann was speechless with rage for a moment. Then she said, "You think your girlfriend's going to win the contest, Marko Lane? Well, lissen up. She's so mean everybody hates her. She hasn't got a real friend in this whole school. If she died, nobody would come to her funeral!"

Derrick looked upset. "Calm down, Ryann. Don't say stuff like that," he told her.

"Well, you're a dog, Ryann," Marko responded. "Woof, woof! Dogs like you don't win beauty contests unless you're gonna compete in a dog show."

Destini grabbed Derrick's hand. "Let's get out of here," she commanded, dragging him after her.

Alonee heard Ryann screaming at Marko and saw Leticia trying to distract her. "I hate you, Marko Lane. And I hate your girlfriend too. I wish you were both dead!"

Marko threw back his head and laughed. "Woof, woof!" he barked before going into a classroom.

Alonee found Ryann on the verge of tears. Leticia was trying to calm her down. Ryann glared at Alonee and said, "I suppose you're going to laugh at me now too. My mother spent a lot of money getting my hair done and a facial. I thought I looked good, but everybody is dissin' me. Now you will too." Ryann had wanted Oliver as her boyfriend. When he chose Alonee, she hated Alonee. But all that was in the past.

"No, you look very nice, Ryann," Alonee assured her. "Your hair is pretty and I like your makeup. Those girls at the cosmetic counters do a great job. Like, I never knew how to apply lipstick and then some cosmetics girl showed me."

Ryann began to whimper. "Marko Lane called me a dog!"

"He's mean to everybody," Alonee said. "You can't take what he says seriously. He loves to insult people."

"Everybody's saying his girlfriend, Jasmine, is so beautiful that she's gonna win Princess of the Fair," Ryann whined. "How could that be? She's as hateful as Marko. Why would we elect somebody like that?"

"I don't think she'll win," Alonee objected.

Suddenly Ryann stared at Alonee. "*You're* pretty. I bet you want to be Princess of the Fair too."

"Uh-uh, Ryann," Alonee protested. "I wouldn't want it if they gave it to me. They won't, but even if they did, I wouldn't want it.

I don't like contests like this. I hate beauty contests. That's what it all gets down to. It's degrading to judge people just on their looks. I see those big beauty pageants on TV. Those girls are herded like cows or sheep at the county fair. It makes me sick."

"But it would be so great to win all those clothes from Lawson's," Ryann said. "And to be a princess and wear the tiara. They'd take pictures and everything. Nothing like that ever happened to me before. It would just be so amazing." Then a forlorn look came to Ryann's face. "And I *am* pretty. *I am*," she insisted.

"Well, good luck, Ryann," Alonee wished her, "See you, Leticia."

As Alonee walked along the pathway to her class, she ran into Ms. Amsterdam. The teacher had recovered from yesterday's encounter with Mr. Pippin. She was again her usual beaming self.

"Hi, Alonee," she called. "Aren't you excited about the princess contest? Everybody's talking about it. It really has brought the campus to life. It was my idea, you know. We had this faculty meeting about how school spirit just wasn't there. We needed to do something. We were brainstorming ideas. Well, I remembered something we did in my high school in Oakland. I ran it up the flagpole, as they say. And the faculty voted for it. Our festival in Oakland was so successful too."

"Oh . . . really?" Alonee replied. She really wanted to say, "It's a stupid idea. I wish you hadn't thought of it because it's already created a lot of hurt feelings." But there was no way Alonee was going to say that and hurt Ms. Amsterdam's feelings.

"You know, Alonee," Ms. Amsterdam went on, "I'm hearing so many good things about you. You're always so willing to pitch in on worthwhile activities and you *are* very lovely. I wouldn't be surprised if you ended up the girl wearing the tiara!" Ms. Amsterdam then giggled like a middle schooler.

"I don't think so," Alonee objected, "but thanks."

"Our kids are a lot deeper than some people give them credit for," Ms. Amsterdam continued. "I think they're going to look deeper than beauty. I just love the students here at Tubman. They aren't a lot of airheads. I have faith in their good judgment."

Alonee didn't agree, but she smiled and walked on. Along her path she noticed several boys with their heads together. Alonee didn't know any of them really well. One of them, Everette Keenan, was in Mr. Pippin's class. He was a good football player and a fair student. Now he was engrossed in saying something to the other boys. Even though she knew it was rude to eavesdrop, she stopped walking near the group to listen.

"I talked to a lot of guys and my list goes like this." Everette was talking to the others and reading from a paper on a clipboard. "There're seven babes on the list. I'm going to start from the bottom. Number seven is Alicia Carr. You know her. She's got the legs that go on forever."

The three other boys laughed at that. Then Everette went on. "Babe number six is Neely Pelham."

"Woo-hoo!" a boy named Vonay howled. "She just six? She should be higher than that."

Everette ignored Vonay and kept going down the list. "Five is Cherie Anders, four is Carissa Polson. Number three is Alonee Lennox. Number two is Jasmine Benson. And numero uno is babe number one, Sereeta Prince."

The boys slapped their thighs, bent over laughing, and made animal sounds. Alonee felt sick to her stomach. She wanted to run to Ms. Amsterdam's classroom and scream at her, "Why did you do this? Why? Why?"

"Wait," Vonay said, "on my list Alicia is six and Neely is four. Neely has a bod to die for."

The boys started laughing again. "You seen some of these ugly chicks thinking they might win?" Vonay chuckled. "They all look like winners at an ugly contest!

Now they're primping up. They think they got a shot at it."

Everette started laughing. "Chick in biology, dudes, she's so ugly she looks like the frog we were dissecting." He lowered his voice and tried to sound like a girl. "She's going, 'I think I might win that princess contest.'"

The four boys almost collapsed laughing. Alonee felt angry and humiliated. But she didn't know what to do with her anger. It was too late to stop the ridicule. It would have to roll on to its conclusion.

When Alonee got home from school, she shared her bitter feelings with her mother. "It's so awful, Mom. Some of the guys are acting like idiots. And some of the girls are making fools of themselves. If only we were just having a fair and we'd skip the princess thing."

"Honey," Mom suggested, "it sounds like homecoming queen or something like that. Nothing wrong with that. Just rise above it."

"But it's already caused terrible feelings," Alonee argued. "I just hate it so much."

"I talked to Monie, Jaris's mother, last night on the phone," Alonee's mother responded. "And she said a lot of kids are looking deeper than just at how pretty a girl is. They're really thinking about what these girls have meant to the school and to each other. You're hearing a few silly boys rating the girls on some stupid chart. But Monie thinks the kids are going to surprise us with their maturity."

"Yeah, right," Alonee said sarcastically.

"Don't be cynical, Alonee," Mom scolded.

The next day, in Ms. Amsterdam's sociology class, she lectured on social norms. "Our behavior is regulated by laws of course, like we cannot run a red light. But social norms guide us just as strictly. Some things we would never do even though there is no law against it. Can someone give me an example?"

31

Alonee raised her hand. "Well, you're sitting in a restaurant. You'd like to drink your soup from the bowl. But, of course, you won't do that."

Ms. Amsterdam smiled and agreed, "Absolutely not!"

Derrick Shaw raised his hand. Everybody knew that Derrick didn't ask insightful questions as a rule. They held their breaths. They all hoped he wouldn't make a fool of himself again.

"There's no law," he began, "that you have to be polite to people. Like, if you're rude, no police officer is gonna arrest you. But when people are rude, it messes up society."

"Yes, Derrick, that's a good observation," Ms. Amsterdam replied.

Ryann raised her hand. "People say mean things to each other all the time. That makes life miserable," she observed.

From the rear of the classroom came the soft but distinct "Woof, woof." Marko Lane looked very serious, though everyone around him knew he had made the noise. His friends were sitting around him, and they snickered. Marko was betting that Ms. Amsterdam wouldn't hear the sounds. Or, he figured, she wouldn't be sure where they came from. Marko was used to doing such things in Mr. Pippin's class. Since Mr. Pippin's hearing was not sharp, usually Marko got away with tricks like that. But Ms. Amsterdam had very good hearing.

Ms. Amsterdam smiled most of the time. Now the smile vanished from her face. "Marko Lane," she asked. "Would you do me a favor?"

"Sure, Ms. Amsterdam," Marko responded, swinging from his desk. He had an easy smile on his face.

"Would you come up here to the front of the room, Marko?" Ms. Amsterdam requested.

"Sure, glad to oblige," Marko agreed. He strolled to the front, looking around and smiling at the other students. "What can I do for you, Ms. Amsterdam?"

"Marko, you can do this for me," Ms. Amsterdam said. "You can be a gentleman. A gentleman does not utter slurs against other people."

"*What*? I didn't—" Marko gasped.

"You did, Marko. I heard you," Ms. Amsterdam told him. "Most of the class heard you. I will not stand for it in my classroom. So, everyone in class, look at this young man standing here. He has provided a good example of how rudeness and unkindness disrupt society. In sociology, we learn about the need for cooperation. The only way a society can benefit us all is for all of us to respect one another. I am asking you, Marko Lane, to give us all that respect. Now, return to your seat."

A faint smile was on Ryann's lips. Marko had been humiliated in front of everybody. Ms. Amsterdam had saved Ryann from embarrassment by not asking who was the butt of the "Woof, woof" sound. Ryann knew, though. She glanced gratefully at the teacher.

At the end of class, Marko stomped out, simmering with rage.

"What a creep that Amsterdam is," he fumed loudly. "She had no right to put me out in front of everybody like that. She violated my rights. She's no teacher. She treats us like a first-grade class. Everybody make nice-nice with each other. What a jerk!"

"You had it coming, Marko," Alonee told him. "We all know you were trying to hurt Ryann. Didn't you see her just now? She got away from here as fast as she could. How could you be so cruel?"

"I was just joking," Marko protested.

"Man, that's a cop-out," Oliver Randall chimed in. "When we hurt somebody, we ought to own up to it. We ought to be man enough to say, 'I'm sorry for acting like a creep.' It's bad enough to do stuff like that to a guy, but to a girl? Haven't you got any class, man?"

Marko turned on Oliver with fire in his eyes. "Who do you think you are, Randall?" he snarled. "You just came to this school.

You came to Tubman out of nowhere. Now you're laying down the law to somebody who's part of this school. You think you're better than everybody else. That's because you got a senile old geezer for a father who tries to teach astronomy at college. He's probably so old and decrepit he can hardly stand up!"

Alonee saw something in Oliver Randall's face that she had never seen. He loved and respected his father. His dad was a highly respected professor at City College. Alonee saw raw, raw anger flame across Oliver's face. She saw his hands tighten into fists. Alonee had seen Oliver angry before, but never like this. He always seemed so controlled, so in charge of his feelings.

Oliver took a step toward Marko. His eyes were wild with hate. Somebody else saw the change too. Kevin Walker was right there and he saw it. Kevin remembered the cruelty Marko had exhibited toward him when he first came to Tubman. He remembered wanting to beat Marko into a bloody pulp. But he stopped just in time. Now it didn't look as if Oliver was going to stop.

Kevin moved swiftly, getting between Oliver and Marko. Oliver tried to shove Kevin out of the way and get to Marko. Kevin grabbed Oliver's forearm and held him. Then he turned to Marko and yelled, "Get your freakin' self out of here, Lane!"

Marko streaked away. He knew this wasn't just an ordinary moment when words would be flung back and forth.

Kevin spoke softly to Oliver. "Easy man. I been there." He relaxed his hold on Oliver's arm. Oliver took a deep breath. He closed, then opened his eyes. He looked at Kevin Walker and said in a husky voice, "Thanks man."

Then Oliver quickly took off.

CHAPTER THREE

A few steps outside Ms. Amsterdam's classroom, Marko ran into more trouble.

"You're making me look bad!" Jasmine screamed at him, as she approached him in the hallway. "You calling that girl a dog in front of everybody. She's a poor little girl from Alabama, and everybody's feeling sorry for her. What's the matter with you, fool? I'm trying to win this Princess of the Fair contest and people're saying, 'Oh, she's no good 'cause she's Marko Lane's girlfriend. She gotta be mean like him or she wouldn't hang with him.' You're spoiling it all for me. I won't stand for it!"

Marko stared at his girlfriend. He'd been catching it from all sides that day. He was sick of it. He didn't need this, not from Jasmine. He treated her like a queen. "Jasmine, don't you be yelling at me," Marko shot back. "I'm good to you, girl. You oughta be on my side. Y'hear what I'm saying?"

"Don't you get it, fool?" Jasmine yelled. "This princess thing is a popularity contest. You're making enemies all over the school. And it's splashing on me like dirty wash water! You're ruining my chances!"

"Jasmine," Marko fumed, "I've done more for you than any guy on this planet has done for his chick. I'm pretty hot myself, girl. I don't need to take this kinda grief from my girl. I could get any girl I wanted at Tubman, and she'd be feelin' lucky to have me. But I'm hangin' with you. You better start to appreciate it, girl, or your man is gonna stray!"

Jasmine put her hands on her hips and stared at Marko. "Oh?" she mimicked his words. "You could get any girl you wanted? Well, maybe you should just go and do that, mister! I want to be Princess of the Fair and get all that publicity. People gonna see the girl who wins on TV. That's gonna lead to big things. I'm pretty enough to go places. I'm not letting you stand in my way."

"Well then, babe, I'll just get out of your way," Marko grinned. "I can do that. There's one pretty little girl named Neely been smiling at me for a long time. I think I'm gonna smile back and see what happens."

Jasmine stalked off and Marko stomped away in another direction.

Alonee was concerned about Oliver, but she couldn't help overhearing the argument. And she couldn't believe what she just saw and heard. Alonee didn't know Neely Pelham very well. But she knew Neely was tall and beautiful, with the perfect figure for modeling. Neely told everyone she wanted to be a model. She had already gotten some small jobs for department store catalogs. She could make any kind of clothing look great.

Alonee got on her cell phone. "Sami," she gushed, "you're not going to believe this. But it looks like Jasmine and Marko just broke up!"

"Get outta here!" Sami cried. "No way those two ever gonna be apart. They go together like peanut butter and jelly."

"Honest, Sami," Alonee insisted. "They had this big fight outside Ms. Amsterdam's classroom. Jasmine really told Marko off. She said the way he treated people was spoiling her chances of being Princess of the Fair. Marko said he didn't have to take that and he could get another girl. He said Neely Pelham's been flirting with him."

"Oh man," Sami exclaimed. "If Marko gets another girl, Jaz is gonna scratch her eyes out when she comes to her senses and sees that Marko's flown the coop."

After her call to Sami, Alonee turned her thoughts to Oliver. Where had he gone? Alonee had been distracted by the battle between Marko and Jasmine. But now she was worried. She figured Oliver must have been bothered that he had lost his cool so badly. He must be disappointed in himself because Kevin had to get between him and Marko.

At lunchtime, Alonee headed for the usual spot under the eucalyptus trees where the posse always gathered. She was hoping Oliver had already arrived, but only Jaris, Sereeta, and Sami were there.

"Anybody see Oliver?" Alonee asked.

Jaris shook his head. "He oughta be along soon," he said.

"It got really ugly in Ms. Amsterdam's class today," Alonee commented. "Marko was making noises like a dog when Ryann was talking. And Ms. Amsterdam really took Marko down."

"Hooray," Jaris exclaimed, "that guy is way outta bounds."

"Then Jasmine and Marko starting fighting," Alonee went on. She didn't want to tell anybody how Oliver almost decked Marko for insulting his father. She didn't want to say anything that would embarrass Oliver.

"This princess deal is really causing trouble," Sereeta remarked. "I ran into Ryann a little while ago and she was still crying. She went to a lot of trouble to make herself pretty. Marko just cut her down. So now she's depressed."

Alonee kept glancing at the paths leading down to their lunch spot. She wanted to see Oliver on one of those paths, but he never showed up. Jaris noticed Alonee looking up the paths and made a suggestion. "Alonee, want me to hunt Oliver down? He said he was working on some science project. So he might be hanging at the library."

"No, that's okay," Alonee said, after checking her cell phone for messages. "I'll catch up to him later." She hoped Oliver wasn't so upset with himself that he went home early.

To everyone's surprise, Jasmine suddenly appeared, coming down the path to the lunch spot. "Hi," Jasmine beamed in a voice very soft and demure for her. "I don't mean to intrude on your private spot. I just wanted to, you know, apologize."

Alonee, Sami, and Jaris exchanged puzzled looks. They were all thinking the same thing. This was a new and kinder Jasmine Benson. She had to polish up her mean girl image and do it fast. "I've been in love with Marko Lane for a while now," Jasmine continued. "He's got his good qualities. There's no doubt of that. He's been good to me. I can't say that he hasn't. He never pushed me around. He never even shoved me once. I wouldn't take that from any guy. But Marko's got a dirty mouth and a mean streak. I guess I pretended it wasn't so 'cause I loved him. Marko, he likes to humiliate people. I see that. I fell in with it too sometimes. I want to apologize for that. I am really sorry, you guys."

Jaris was plucking blades of grass, looking down intently. Sereeta looked pained. Alonee tried to look interested while Jasmine was speaking. But Sami blurted, "Girl, how come you just now come to the new way of lookin' at this stuff?"

"Well," Jasmine explained. "It was something that happened in the Ninety-Nine-Cent and More store. Derrick was working there. And Marko started making fun of him like he does. I joined in. I'm ashamed to admit that, but I did. We were like taunting Derrick that he's too dumb to read real books. So he reads, you know, baby books. Well, Derrick didn't get mad. He just said to me that I was pretty and smart. Why did I need to humiliate people like him? It got me to thinking. I decided I'd do better. So that's why I'm apologizing for stuff I might have done."

"Well, thanks for saying that, Jasmine," Alonee replied. She didn't know if Jasmine was really sorry. She might have been just trying to look better so that she could win the princess contest. But Alonee would give her the benefit of the doubt.

"Yes, thanks," Sereeta said too.

"So," Jaris said, "you and Marko breaking up?"

"I read the boy the riot act," Jasmine answered with a little smile. "I scared that

45

dude outta his wits. He said he can find himself another chick, but he doesn't mean that. He's crazy in love with me. He's gonna go somewhere and sulk. Then he'll come crawling back. I'll take him back, but I got conditions. He's gotta be nicer to people. That's the rule now. No more making fun of people just to get a cheap laugh from his no-good friends. Well, anyways, I hope you guys forgive me."

"Sure," Alonee replied. Jaris and Sereeta mumbled something. Sami said, "We all do bad sometimes."

When Jasmine was gone, Jaris commented, "Boy, if she's going to apologize to every kid Marko hurt, she's got her work cut out for her. She's gonna be busy. But the vote for Princess of the Fair isn't for a while yet, so she has time."

"So you think it's just that, huh, Jaris?" Alonee asked. "She wants votes. She's not really sorry about what she and Marko have done."

"I guess it's possible she's sorry," Jaris conceded. "I guess maybe it's possible for it to snow in July too."

Sami looked thoughtful. She finished her ham and cheese sandwich and declared, "We need to give the chick a chance." Jasmine and Marko had probably insulted Sami more than anybody at Tubman High. Sami always gave back in kind because she wasn't going to be pushed around. But all the fat jokes and all the insults had to hurt. "Maybe she got this idea to be kinder 'cause of the princess thing," Sami continued. "But then maybe it got into her heart that it's something she oughta do anyway. People can change. My daddy always says you gotta give people the chance to do better. Or else there's no such thing as repentance and getting better."

Sereeta looked at Sami and spoke. "I remember a long time ago I was gonna go out on a date with Marko. He seemed nice and exciting. And he is handsome. But you know, Sami, you called me up and talked me out of it. If I'd gone, it would have been such a disaster. Marko was already talking trash with his friends about me. I remember you saying, "We girls got to stick together," and that just sunk into my heart. Sami, you're like one of the most real people on this whole campus. I respect what you say. And I respect what you're saying right now about giving Jasmine another chance. I'm going to go with that, Sami.

Sami smiled at Sereeta and said, "Yeah, it's important for us girls to stick together. And us guys too." She reached over and squeezed Jaris's hand. "We all in this together, dudes."

After lunch, Alonee went looking for Oliver. She found him just where Jaris said he'd probably be, in the library printing up his science report.

"Hi," Alonee whispered. "Missed you at lunch."

"I'm sorry," Oliver apologized in a hushed voice, "I should have told you I needed to do this."

As they walked out of the library together, Oliver reached out and took Alonee's hand. "I could have done the science report tomorrow," he admitted.

"Oh," Alonee said.

"But then," Oliver continued, "I would have had to face you sooner. And I'd have to explain why I turned into such a hot-headed idiot. Kevin saved me from maybe doing serious damage to Marko. I can't remember a time I was so angry. When I saw Marko leering at me and insulting my dad like that, I just went ballistic. I hope you're not disappointed, Alonee."

"I am," Alonee replied, "because now I know you're human. It was so fascinating to believe you came from another planet, like Marko said when you first came to Tubman. I always wanted to date an ET. But now I know you're human and that's okay, because humans are nice too. And you're especially nice."

Oliver pulled Alonee gently against him and kissed her.

That night at home, Alonee helped her mother make chocolate chip cookies for the bake sale at Pastor Bromley's church. The proceeds were going to help with the expenses of the foster children program. Mom was carefully dropping the cookies onto the baking sheet. Her chocolate chip cookies were the best of any at the bake sales. Alonee's mother said that was because she was always a stay-at-home mom. She developed the cooking and baking skills that working mothers didn't have time for.

"Mom," Alonee commented, "I can't figure out why Marko is so mean. Today Jasmine said she was going to try to be nicer because she doesn't like it when he acts that way. I mean, he's got parents who love him. What's wrong with him?"

"We can't always figure things out, honey," Mom answered. "People are a lot harder to figure out than cookies. With cookies, you put in the right ingredients and they come out good all the time. With people, you never can tell. Sometimes parents put in all the love and attention on a child. Then that child comes out sour and mean. And sometimes a child gets battered around by life and still comes out with a good heart."

"Like Sereeta," Alonee noted. "She's been so hurt by what's happened at home. But she goes and helps the foster kids and she's so nice."

"I wouldn't be surprised if Sereeta won that Princess of the Fair contest," Alonee's mother remarked. "She's a beautiful girl and generous too. Might be a lot of kids will feel sorry for her and vote for her for that reason too."

"Yeah, but she doesn't want to win," Alonee objected. "She said she'd give the tiara back if she won."

"Yeah," Mom said, "she's saying that. But if she won, I'm sure it would touch her heart so much that the kids voted for her. Of course, she's not the kind of a girl who's grasping for the prize. But that's just the kind of a girl who *should* win."

After the cookies were finished baking and were stored in tins, Alonee went to her room. As she went online to do some research for English, she decided to look up the Tubman High School Web site. The news there was all about the upcoming fair and the Princess of the Fair contest. There were cute graphics showing clowns and court jesters. Ms. Amsterdam put a message on the fair's Web page:

Who is the Tubman High School junior girl? She is lovely and vivacious. She cares about others. She has great school spirit and gets excited about all our activities. She cares about others. She is the shoulder you cry on. She high-fives you when you win. She's your friend, win or lose. She has the heart of the magnificent lady for whom our school is named, Harriet Tubman. Such a girl will be voted the Princess of the Fair. We shall all be proud

of her. Be sure to vote and vote with
your heart.

Alonee hated what Everette Keenan
and those other boys had been doing,
rating girls like racehorses. But curiosity
got the better of her. She wanted to know
what the girls on that stupid list looked
like. Alonee flipped open last year's
Tubman High yearbook. The really nice
pictures were of the seniors. But the
pictures of the juniors, as well as those of
the freshman and sophomores, were good
too. This year's juniors were sophomores
last year. You could see what they looked
like.

She started looking through the pictures, coming first to the photograph of
Neely Pelham. She was the girl Marko
claimed would be his next girlfriend. Even
as a sophomore, Neely was striking.
Carissa Polson, Kevin's girlfriend, was
cute. When Alonee came to *her* own
picture, she thought she looked like a
little girl. She giggled at it. But Sereeta

Prince was stunning. Jasmine was beautiful too.

Mom was right, Alonee thought. Sereeta would win, and she would be gracious enough to accept it. And in her heart she would be proud and happy.

CHAPTER FOUR

On Friday, just before Ms. McDowell's American history class began, everyone was whispering about the princess contest. Ms. McDowell had to call the class to order twice before the noise ended. She usually didn't have to do that in her classroom. Usually the students needed only to see her at her desk to quiet down. "We're very keyed up today, aren't we?" Ms. McDowell commented wryly. "I hope that reflects your enthusiasm in talking about the 1996 elections and what they meant to our country."

Just then Ms. McDowell noticed a boy in the rear of the room passing out something. He looked like he was handing out wallet-sized photos. "Everette," Ms. McDowell said, "would you bring those cards to me? Please collect those you have already passed out and bring them here."

"It's nothing, Ms. McDowell," Everette replied.

"Please, just collect them all and bring them to me, Everette," the teacher insisted.

The boy reluctantly collected the cards and brought them to Ms. McDowell. They were professional glamour shots of Neely Pelham. Neely looked stunning. Printed on the backs of the photos was the advice to "Vote for Neely Pelham for Princess of the Fair."

"Everette," Ms McDowell explained, "I believe Ms. Amsterdam made the rules very clear. There was to be no campaigning for this contest. These cards are a violation of the rules, and I intend to confiscate them. Where did you get them?"

"Uh," Everette hesitated, "some guy just handed them to me and said to pass them along."

"Oh? A student here?" Ms. McDowell asked.

"Yeah, but I didn't know him. He was a sophomore I think. I'm sorry, Ms. McDowell. I didn't know it was against the rules." Everette sounded contrite.

Alonee remembered that Everette was one of the boys having a high old time rating the girls. Even if he got the cards from Neely, he clearly would not admit it and get her in trouble.

"Everybody," Ms. McDowell announced. "Don't be doing this, please. You are harming the spirit of the fair. It's supposed to be lighthearted and fun. We'll even have some well-respected charities selling T-shirts. So we don't want to have any rivalry."

Ms. McDowell then launched into a discussion of the 1996 election. "There was little doubt that the president would be reelected. Why was that?"

"Presidents in office usually get reelected unless the economy is bad," Alonee answered.

"Yeah," Oliver added. "When people got jobs and money to spend, they feel good about the government. They don't want to change it."

"That's right," Ms. McDowell said. "Other issues count, of course. But no recent president has been denied a second term when the economy was good."

After class, Ms. McDowell went over to the Renaissance fair poster on the bulletin board and highlighted the words "No campaigning of any kind."

Alonee walked from class with Oliver. She overheard Everette talking about the incident.

"Marko Lane gave me those cards," Everette was telling his friend.

"No way!" the other boy said. "His girlfriend's Jasmine Benson."

"Not no more," Everette replied. "He wants to make sure Jasmine loses. So he's promoting Neely. Me and Marko and some girls went to a club last night. Neely was with Marko. They were all over each other.

Marko's father got the cards printed real fast so we could spread them all over Tubman today."

"Neely is smokin' hot," the other boy remarked. "I think I'll vote for her."

As Alonee was crossing the campus to go to English class, she saw Jasmine standing alone. She had one of Neely's publicity pictures in her hand. "What's this all about?" she held up the card to Alonee. "This trash is all over the school. This is a crock. We're not supposed to be doing this. It's not fair. Where does this little witch Neely get off pulling something like this?"

"Yeah," Alonee agreed, "they were trying to pass them out in history. Ms. McDowell grabbed them all and put them in the wastebasket. She said it was against the rules."

"How'd they get this done so fast?" Jasmine wondered. "They're good-quality stuff. Musta cost a lot of money. Neely's just a junior like us with a job at the yogurt store. Where'd she get the money to print all these? That's what I'd like to know."

Alonee knew the answer. But she didn't want to hurt Jasmine even more. Jasmine was thinking her quarrel with Marko would soon be patched up. Marko, though, was serious about the split. He had already gotten his father to help him hurt his old girlfriend. Marko had a lot of pride. He didn't mind ridiculing other people and crushing their pride. But Jasmine made a big mistake bawling him out in public, where his friends could see him being dissed by his girlfriend.

"These pictures," Jasmine complained, "they don't even look like Neely. She wants to be a model. She had these pictures taken someplace where they fix you up to look like a movie star. This is so not fair!"

When Oliver walked into Mr. Pippin's English class, he didn't even look in Marko's direction. You could tell by the expression on Oliver's face that he probably would never forget Marko's insult. Alonee understood. She would have felt the same way if somebody insulted her father.

Mr. Pippin hadn't come in yet. Derrick grinned at Kevin Walker and asked him a question. "You gonna vote for Carissa? Seems a guy should vote for his own girl-friend?"

Kevin nodded. "Oh sure," he said. "I'll vote for Carissa. But she doesn't think she'll win. She doesn't care too much either way. That suits me. I'd hate to have a girlfriend who's all stressed out about the contest."

"I'm voting for Destini," Derrick replied. "But she's just laughing it off. I think she's real cute. But she says nobody but me is gonna vote for her!"

Jasmine came into the classroom and made a point of sitting next to Ryann. She wanted everyone to see how she sympa-thized with Ryann. Jasmine wanted others to know she didn't like Marko's cruel taunts. Jasmine wanted to show everyone the new Jasmine Benson. She was a friend of the underdog and kind to victims of verbal abuse. "So, how you doin', Ryann? You look really good today," Jasmine commented.

"Oh, thanks," Ryann responded, a puzzled look on her face.

Jasmine didn't even glance at Marko, who was sitting farther back. She believed that the longer she gave him the cold shoulder, the more sorry he'd be when he crawled back. Jasmine believed Marko really regretted the things he had said to her, especially the part about getting a new girlfriend. Jasmine knew deep down that Marko loved her. He could never turn his back on her. He could never be happy with someone else.

"Ryann," Jasmine spoke quietly. "I'm really sorry Marko was mean to you. I told him I wouldn't stand for that anymore. And another thing. If I've ever said anything to hurt you, Ryann, I'm sorry about that too. I'm really trying to be a better person. I believe people can change, don't you?"

"What?" Ryann was taken aback. "Are you making a joke or something?"

"No, I'm really serious," Jasmine insisted.

Mr. Pippin came in then and began his class. "We are starting a unit on nonfiction," he announced. "We shall be discussing some articles in the textbook on the process of thinking." He turned toward his bulletin board when he heard some of the students snickering. He spotted one of Neely Pelham's photos sticking to the board with a red pushpin. He ripped it down and sent the red push pin flying.

"What is this?" Mr. Pippin demanded. "Who is this?"

"It's Neely Pelham," Ryann answered in a wounded voice. Ryann knew her chances of winning were worse with Neely Pelham in the race. "She's a really pretty junior. She had a million of her pictures printed. Now she's passing them out all over the school. It's not fair, Mr. Pippin. Every girl should have an equal chance to be Princess of the Fair. We were told not to campaign and I haven't. I could have made some cute posters about me and stuff. But I didn't. Now she's getting away with this and getting ahead of the rest of us. Don't you think that's really wrong, Mr. Pippin?"

Mr. Pippin looked like he was going to have some kind of attack. He glared at Ryann and declared, "I don't care about any of this. I think it is all idiocy. I want nothing to do with it. Don't *anyone* ever dare to deface my bulletin board with any reminders of that stupid contest."

Mr. Pippin slowly caught his breath then. He glanced at Marko Lane, who was smirking. "Does something amuse you, Marko?" Mr. Pippin asked in a sarcastic tone.

"No sir, I'm just in a good mood today," he replied.

Mr. Pippin then began discussing the Robert M. Hutchins article, "That Candles May Be Brought."

"Here is an essay," he lectured, "that speaks to the need to think things through. Thinking is painful. It is more popular just to accept what the loudest voices around us are saying. But we must have the courage to think, to find the truth."

Ryann Kern raised her hand shakily.

"Yes, Ryann," Mr. Pippin acknowledged her. "Have you a comment on the essay we are discussing?"

"I just think it's very unfair that Neely Pelham can spread her pictures around and we can't campaign," she said.

"We are not talking about the ridiculous princess hogwash now," Mr. Pippin snapped. "We are talking about the serious issues of our time."

Alonee caught Oliver hiding his smile behind his hand again. But Oliver recovered enough to respond to Mr. Pippin's point. "When you ask people why they hold certain opinions, they often can't give you a good reason. They'll say some guy on the radio said so and they're going along with him."

"Exactly," Mr. Pippin replied gratefully. Sometimes, but not often, a student exceeded Mr. Pippin's expectations. . . .

The students filed from the room after the class ended. Marko worked his way through the crowd so that he was walking beside Jasmine. She smiled a little when she saw him. She was deciding what she would say when he pleaded with her to take him back and forgive him. She wouldn't let him off easy. But she would give him some hope. She didn't want to crush the boy. And if the truth be told, she did still love him, with all his faults. Marko would have to assure her that he would curb his nasty mouth. He would have to promise not to hurt her chances to win the princess title. Then she might consent to go out with him.

"I'm taking you out, babe," Marko announced.

"Not so fast, boy," Jasmine replied with a half smile on her full, red lips. "You ain't taking me nowhere until we get some things straight. It ain't gonna be business as usual, if you hear what I'm saying."

"No, babe," Marko explained, "you're misunderstanding me. I'm not saying take you out like on a date. I am saying take you down off your high horse." There was an almost evil sound to Marko's words. He looked at Jasmine with his dark eyes, which could be warm and merry. But now they were clouded and sinister.

"What're you talkin' about, fool?" Jasmine demanded.

"You got a lot of goodies from me, girl," Marko snarled. "All the pretty sparkly things, the gold chains, the hot dates, and all that. Nobody does that and then dumps me in front of everybody, with my friends lookin' on. Nobody stands there and yells at me and cuts me down with everybody watching. I am taking you *out* girl. I built you up with all the pretty things. Now I am breakin' you down. I am gonna make you one sorry chick for what you done to me."

Jasmine's eyes grew very wide and then she hissed at Marko. "Don't you dare threaten me, you big fool! Everybody knows what you are. They didn't need me to tell them. You can ask anybody. They hate you, Marko Lane. And their hate is spilling over on me like a dirty, greasy cloud of poison. It ain't happenin' anymore. Don't you ever come near me again. You hear me? You crawl back under whatever rock you've been under, Marko Lane. You slither around down there with the bugs and the snakes and the other slimy things like you. 'Cause that's where you belong."

Clutching her books to her chest, Jasmine ran from the front of the English building. She kept on running until she reached the grassy area where the posse ate lunch under the eucalyptus trees. There was nobody there now.

Jasmine flung herself onto the ground. Her books went flying. She lay on the grass sobbing, her shoulders and her whole body heaving.

"Get a load of her," Destini pointed out to Derrick, who was walking with her. "That's Jasmine Benson having a fit over there. Somebody musta given her what she's always giving out. Look at her bawling over there. She can dish it out, but she can't take it."

"Man," Derrick remarked, "she looks in bad shape. Should we do something maybe?"

"No, Derrick," Destini responded. "You know what that girl did to me? When I was dating Tyron, he was really jealous, crazy jealous. Jasmine would see me in really innocent situations with other guys, like camping out with the foster kids with you. Jasmine would lie and tell Tyron that me and these boys were doing stuff together behind his back. Tyron would go ballistic. Jasmine lied about me just to make trouble. I hated her so much 'cause she'd get Tyron so mad he'd hurt me—*really* hurt me. I mean, like my mom says, 'Whatever goes around comes around.' So whatever happened to her, she had it coming." With that, Destini grasped Derrick's hand and they hurried away.

Some other students came along. A few laughed to see Jasmine sobbing on the ground. Fewer still were actually happy to see her in trouble. But most of the students passed by, saw Jasmine, and then just walked on without giving her much thought.

Sami Archer was usually with another student as she walked around the campus. She had a lot of friends. As often as not, other girls, or even boys, were telling her their problems in the hopes she might help. And she often did. Sami was rarely alone. But now she was walking by herself and doing some last-minute cramming for a test that afternoon.

Sami happened to glance over under the eucalyptus trees. She saw Jasmine thrashing around and crying. Sami's first thought was that Jasmine had hurt somebody again. And now they'd gotten even, and she was feeling sorry for herself.

Sami remembered the worst encounter she ever had with Jasmine. The cheerleader car wash money went missing. Jasmine was trying to blame Sereeta Prince. Jasmine and Sami argued. Jasmine ended up calling Sami's mother insulting names. Sami punched Jasmine in the face because nobody dissed Sami's mother. The bitter fight might have turned a lot uglier if Jaris hadn't stepped in. Jaris and some others broke up the fight. But Sami could still remember Jasmine screaming at her. "Sami Archer, if you ever hit me again, I swear I'll break your fat neck!" Sami remembered the hatred she felt for Jasmine that day and the other days when Jasmine had hurt her or hurt someone she loved.

Sami stood there, staring at Jasmine as she rolled back and forth dramatically, like something dying. One time, Sami remembered, she saw a big crow hit by a car. The bird was flung into a field, where it thrashed on the ground. Its big wings flapped desperately and uselessly. It was trying to will itself to somehow rise from the ground and fly away from its pain and terror. Sami had run into the field to try to rescue the crow. Before she could get to it, the bird had grown mercifully quiet in death. Sami buried the crow that day and went home.

Almost against her will now, Sami walked toward the girl who was sobbing on the ground.

"Jasmine," she said, "it can't be that bad, can it?" Sami slowly approached her.

Jasmine stopped tossing and sat up slightly. Her makeup was smeared all over her face. She looked almost comical. On closer inspection, she looked ghoulish with the green eye shadow running down her cheeks. Jasmine stared at Sami as she would have looked at a ghost.

Sami came closer. She sat down on the grass beside Jasmine. "Take it easy, girl," she said soothingly.

Jasmine started sobbing again, convulsively. Sami reached out and took the girl in her arms, patting her on the back. "Ain' nothin' that bad, girl," Sami calmed her. "What's the matter?"

"He's e-evil . . . h-he's cruel and e-evil," Jasmine finally gasped.

"You be talkin' 'bout Marko?" Sami asked. She knew about the troubles between

Jasmine and Marko. Apparently they had worsened.

"Y-yes . . . he's so mean and evil," Jasmine sobbed. She wiped her tears and more of her makeup off with the back of her hand.

"Well, girl," Sami commented, "tell me somethin' I don't know. We been seein' that for a long time now. He just like to hurt people."

"I was so . . . s-so stupid," Jasmine cried, pulling herself together. "I thought he loved me. But now . . . now he threatened me. He said he was going to ruin everything for me. He can do it too. His father is very powerful. I've seen his father do things." She shuddered.

"He can't ruin you, Jasmine," Sami assured her. "He just a big-mouthed sucka. His daddy too. He just a stuffed shirt walkin' around in gold chains. Come on now, stop your cryin'. Gonna be okay. You ain't dyin'. You ain't sick. You got a mama and a daddy who love you to pieces. Everything cool.

Forget about that big old sucka. Let him stew in his own juice."

Jasmine took a long, deep breath. She looked Sami in the eye and tried to make a joke. "I bet I look a mess, huh? I'd never get elected Princess of the Fair looking like this, would I?" She almost smiled a little, though her lower lip quivered.

Sami smiled too. "You got that right, girl. You look like one of those clowns on the posters."

Jasmine giggled nervously.

Sami helped Jasmine get to her feet. They walked over to the restroom. Sami spent about fifteen minutes helping Jasmine restore her face. She had to wash all the old goop off and apply new makeup.

"It *will* be all right, won't it?" Jasmine said. "You're right, Sami. I don't need him. I'm strong."

"You gotta be strong to make it in this world, girl," Sami declared.

"Uh . . . Sami . . . thanks for, you know . . ." Jasmine's voice trailed off.

"Oh, nothin' to it, sister," Sami said. "We girls gotta stick together, right?"

"Right," Jasmine agreed in a husky voice. She stared at Sami, confused by all that had happened. She couldn't find the words to express what she was thinking. Why had Sami Archer reached out to her? Jasmine had never given Sami any reason to like her or even not to dislike her. Jasmine said nothing about the thoughts swirling in her mind. And the two girls walked together to their sociology class.

CHAPTER FIVE

As Alonee started her walk home that day, Neely Pelham came along. She always looked beautiful, but today she was extra lovely. She wore a black turtleneck sweater with a new gold chain that Alonee had never seen on her. Alonee wasn't in the same classes with Neely. But sometimes they met and talked at school games or dances.

"That's a beautiful gold chain, Neely," Alonee noted.

"It's a gift from Marko," Neely explained. "He's so generous."

"How nice," Alonee said without meaning.

"I saw you riding in a BMW with your boyfriend, Alonee," Neely commented. "He must be rich."

"The car belongs to his father," Alonee responded. "And it's an old BMW. You can get them cheap after a few years."

"I'm really getting excited about the Princess of the Fair contest," Neely said. "You too?"

"No, I'm not into things like that," Alonee replied.

"Well, I'm not into it either, not the idea of being Princess of the Fair," Neely agreed, "but it could lead to other things. The local TV will cover it. And who knows who might see it? They're always looking for fresh new faces. I've been in beauty pageants since I was two years old. And I won a couple of them. I was Miss Skateboard when I was twelve. Some store was putting it on. And I was Miss Sandy Cove Beach when I was fourteen. That was the best. I'd love to be a model. I think that has to be the most exciting thing in the whole world."

Neely looked at Alonee and noted, "*You're* very pretty. Have you ever been in a beauty contest?"

Alonee laughed. "Oh my gosh, no! Mom would think I was crazy. My dad would ground me."

"But seriously, Alonee," Neely persisted, "the guys are taking polls, you know, of what girls are likely to get a lot of votes. I've seen some of the polls. You're in the top ten on all of them. I'm in there too, but you're more popular around here. You have a lot of friends. You could win, Alonee."

Just then, Alonee saw Oliver's father arriving in the visitor's parking lot. In a few minutes Oliver would be coming to ride home with his dad. "See you, Neely," Alonee said abruptly. Then she turned and walked over to the BMW. "Hi, Mr. Randall, how are you?" she greeted him.

Oliver Randall's seventy-year-old father smiled warmly. "Just fine," he responded.

"I've finished an enjoyable day of teaching astronomy to students who love it almost as much as I do. I feel guilty to have the chance to share what I know with interested adults. I feel a lot of sympathy and admiration for the high school teachers trying to cram stuff into teenager's heads, when many of the kids couldn't care less. That must be hard."

"We have a teacher here," Alonee said, "Mr. Pippin. Maybe Oliver has told you about him."

"Oh yes indeed," Mr. Randall replied. "I knew him when he was an undergraduate at UCLA. I met him through the fraternity. Poor fellow, bless his heart. It must be terrible to be so discouraged with a job and still be doing it. . . . Oh, here comes my boy. Alonee, Oliver and I wondered if you'd like to join us. Tonight is frozen yogurt night."

Oliver arrived and asked, "Has Dad talked you into yogurt night? It would just be a half hour, forty-five minutes. You got the time, Alonee?"

Alonee pulled out her cell phone and called home. "Mom, I'll be about an hour late tonight, okay?"

"Oliver, huh?" Mom inquired.

"Yeah," Alonee giggled. "I'll be coming home in style, via a BMW."

Alonee, Oliver, and Mr. Randall drove off toward a new frozen yogurt shop. It served sweet and tart frozen yogurt with over a hundred topping choices.

Mr. Randall started to drive. He spoke to his son. "I was just telling Alonee how fortunate I feel to be teaching astronomy to students who actually like the subject. Some of your poor teachers don't have that luxury. Another thing too—not so much age discrimination against old college teachers. Elderly high school teachers have it rougher." He chuckled.

"Yeah," Oliver agreed, "they give Mr. Pippin a hard time because he's nearing retirement."

"Retirement! What an obscene word," Mr. Randall sighed. "I shall never retire.

Retiring from work you love is like retiring from life."

Oliver laughed and said to Alonee, "See what a great dad I've got? No rocking chair for him." Alonee detected something a bit sad in Oliver's eyes, even though he was laughing. What Marko had said continued to hurt him. It would maybe always hurt him. That was the worst part of cruel words. They never died. Instead they crawled into your memory bank and crept out again, over and over, to taunt you.

"You know, Alonee," Mr. Randall went on, "when I was young, I saw a lot of racial discrimination. Oliver has never seen what people of my generation have seen. Same for you, Alonee. You've seen films of it. But it's not the same as actually seeing it in real time. We have to thank brave people like Dr. Martin Luther King Jr. and all those marchers of the 1950s and 1960s. It's not legal or cool to be racially prejudiced any-more. But now there's age discrimination. That's acceptable, but not to me. When a stranger says to me, 'Hi, pop,' I respond by saying, 'Oh, I am so sorry. Are you my son? I forgot I had a son who looks like you.'"

"That's funny," Alonee giggled.

They pulled into the parking lot and walked into the shop. After sampling the tart yogurt, Alonee ordered chocolate. Oliver and his father got strawberry yogurt. "Probably has as many calories as ice cream. I delude myself into thinking it's health food," Mr. Randall remarked.

As they finished their yogurt, Mr. Randall turned to Alonee and said, "I understand the Princess of the Fair contest is in full swing. How's that going?"

"Really ugly," Alonee replied. "One of the girls—Neely Pelham—got her boyfriend to pass out glamour shots of her with little messages urging people to vote for her."

"And this isn't kosher, right?" Mr. Randall asked.

"No," Alonee affirmed. She looked at Oliver. "Marko did it."

"Marko Lane, eh?" Mr. Randall noted. "Son, isn't he the boy who thought you were from Mars?"

"Yeah," Oliver answered. "I'd like to send him on a one-way trip to Mars."

A questioning look appeared in Mr. Randall's eyes, but he said nothing. Of course, Oliver had never said anything about almost punching Marko out for the "a senile old geezer" remark. Oliver would never tell Mr. Randall about the remark because he would only hurt his father by repeating the slur. Nor was Oliver proud of how he had reacted afterward. Except for Kevin Walker's intervention, he could have done something very dangerous. But Mr. Randall was very close to his son. He perceived in Oliver's sudden tense look that there was big-time bad blood between him and this Marko Lane.

As they walked to the BMW, Alonee asked, "Mr. Randall, when you drop me off at my house, could you come in for a minute and meet my parents? Dad's home tonight. I know he'd love to meet you."

"Splendid," Mr. Randall replied.

After parking the BMW in the Lennox driveway, Mr. Randall walked to the door with Oliver and Alonee. Mom answered: "Oh!" She gave a delighted little cry. "Floyd, Alonee brought Oliver and his dad!"

Alonee's father appeared quickly, extending his hand. "Alonee has told us all about you, Mr. Randall. You teach astronomy, eh? I was fascinated by astronomy as a boy. I wanted to be an astronaut and visit the moon—or be a firefighter. Alonee has probably told you what won out!"

"Yes, I know all about Alonee's father being a firefighter," Mr. Randall responded. "Thank God for you people. When I see flames, I'm running away from them. I thank God Almighty there are brave people running toward the fire!"

"And this is my mom," Alonee made the introduction.

"She makes amazing pumpkin pie, Dad," Oliver interjected. "The other night I think I ate the whole pie."

Mr. Randall and Oliver stayed only a couple of minutes. They politely declined the invitation to come into the living room and sit for a while. When they left, Alonee asked her parents, "Well, what did you think of Oliver's dad?"

"A nice, elegant man," Mom commented. "When I invited him over for Sunday dinner some weekend, he promised to come. Oliver has good roots."

"And he appreciates firefighters," Floyd Lennox laughed. "That counts in my book."

At Tubman High the next morning, the campaign to pass out more glamour photos of Neely Pelham went underground. As Alonee was going to and from classes, three were shoved into her hand. The newer poses looked even less like the real Neely Pelham. The campaign was against the rules. But nobody could stop it.

"You mean this babe goes to Tubman?" one boy asked in amazement. "Where is she? I've never seen her."

"She doesn't look exactly like that," Alonee objected. "The camera doesn't lie. But it can fib a little."

At lunchtime, Alonee met up with Marko and Neely, who was close beside him. He wasn't throwing barbs at anybody as he often did. He was very polite.

"Hey Alonee," he called in a cordial voice, "this girl here is Princess of the Fair."

Neely giggled, "Nothing's decided yet."

"It's gonna happen, babe," Marko assured her. He looked at Alonee then. "No offense, Alonee, 'cause you're pretty too. But you, you're not ambitiative like Neely is. This girl's gonna be Miss Universe one day. That's the truth. Remember, you heard it first from Marko Lane."

"Well, good luck to you, Neely," Alonee said.

"Thanks," she replied, her gold chains sparkling as she walked away on Marko's arm.

Alonee continued to her locker to get her English book. She noticed a strange odor in the hall. It smelled like something had died.

"What's that?" Derrick exclaimed. "Phew!"

"It seems to be coming from Jasmine's locker," Alonee pointed out. "We better call the office. The maintenance guys have to get in there and find out what's causing that stench!"

Isaac, the head of maintenance, and two other men arrived. A crowd of students had gathered to watch the opening of the locker. At the very moment they sprung open the locker door, Jasmine arrived. Horror came over her face. "What happened to my locker?" she screamed.

"Somebody stuck an old, moldy chicken sandwich in there, missy," Isaac explained. "Nothing smells worse than old chicken leftovers after a couple days in the heat."

"But . . . why . . . who—who would do that?" Jasmine gasped.

"Somebody who don't like you much, missy," Isaac suggested. "Who knows your locker combination besides you?"

"Nobody but—" Jasmine began to say her boyfriend. She stopped herself. "I don't know," she said instead.

Alonee used to hear Jasmine saying how she and Marko stuck love notes in each other's lockers. Alonee had little doubt Marko had pulled the prank. He was really mad at Jasmine.

Isaac cleaned up the mess. Then he advised, "Don't be giving out your combination to people. Some guys have a sick sense of humor."

"I'm sorry, Jasmine," Alonee said. "That was a creepy thing for someone to do."

Jasmine's eyes burned with anger. "He did it," she seethed. "Marko Lane did it. I remember one time in middle school he had it in for two guys. He kept some old chicken at home and left it rotting until it was good and smelly. Then he brought it to school and stuck it in their lunch boxes. That's the kind of thing he does. He thinks it's funny. But it's nothin' but sick."

"If you know it's Marko, you should tell security," Alonee told her.

"He'd just deny it," Jasmine said. "I couldn't prove it anyway. This is his way of trying to break me down. He wants me to get upset so I'll stop trying to win that contest that means so much to me. But I got news for that fool. I'm more determined than ever to win. And I got some new ideas to help me win. Marko Lane is gonna be surprised when they announce the Princess of the Fair is Jasmine Benson!" With that, Jasmine stalked off.

Jaris, Oliver, and Alonee shared looks.

"She's got some new ideas to win the contest?" Jaris wondered. "What is that supposed to mean? This is getting crazy."

"Jaris," Alonee asked, "do you remember when we were twelve in middle school and they had this medieval thing—Ye Olde

English Festival? They elected a king and a queen?"

"Yeah," Jaris replied, grinning. "You and I won, Alonee. I got to wear this velvet cape and the crown. You had a tiara. It was pretty cool. I still have the pictures of you and me in our royal outfits."

"Me too!" Alonee cried. "I showed them to my little sister the other day."

"So how did you guys win," Oliver asked. "Did the kids vote?"

"No," Alonee laughed. "We had to collect recyclable cans and bottles. The boy and girl who collected the most cans won. I can still remember Jaris and me hauling those sticky garbage bags filled with cola cans. We must have brought in a million cans."

"At least," Jaris said with a shudder.

"That would have been a good way to pick the Princess of the Fair," Oliver remarked. "Then we wouldn't be having all this nonsense."

At midday, more and more of Neely Pelham's photos showed up. Some kids looked at the pictures and tossed them, not always in the trash barrels. A countercampaign began to take shape. The supporters of the other girls were defacing Neely's photographs. Many of her pictures sported a big moustache. Others showed a red clown's nose over her small, lovely nose. Unflattering jingles appeared on the backs of some of the photos.

"Neely, Neely, ugly really," one jingle read.

Ryann stood looking at some of the disfigured photos. "Aren't these a scream?" she laughed. "Look, here she's got a snaggle tooth. Did you guys see this one? She has a fang!" Ryann had nothing in particular against Neely Pelham except that she seemed to be competing unfairly. To Ryann, the counter campaign seemed like perfect justice.

Marko Lane came along as Ryann and Leticia were comparing disfigured photos. They were howling with glee, "Look Ryann," Leticia howled, laughing hysterically.

"This one has her with green hair and horns coming out of her head!"

"This is the funniest one," Ryann said. "Some of her teeth are blacked out and she looks like a hobo!"

Marko glared at Ryann. "What's so funny, dogface?" he sneered. "Neely's so beautiful that those dirty tricks they're doin' to her picture won't make no difference. If they make real photographs of you, they'd scare the children."

"Everybody's making a fool out of your girlfriend, Marko Lane," Ryann crowed. "Everybody's laughing at Neely. She's never gonna win now. She's a laughingstock!"

Marko ripped one of the disfigured photos from Ryann's hand. Ryann and Leticia laughed all the harder. "There's too many of them now," Ryann screamed. "It's the hottest collector's item on campus."

During lunchtime, Alonee saw about five arguments over the Princess of the Fair contest and over the photographs. Some kids were tearing up the good ones. Others were trying to get hold of and destroy the others.

"You know what, Oliver?" Alonee declared. "We've got to talk to Ms. Amsterdam. The voting isn't for another several days. Maybe there's time to change the way it's done."

"I think it's too late. We could try," Oliver agreed.

After lunch, they walked to Ms. Amsterdam's classroom. When classes were not being held, Mr. Pippin locked his classroom. Students could see him sitting in there working. But he didn't want to be bothered. You had to make an appointment to see him. But both Ms. McDowell and Ms. Amsterdam were always available to the students.

When Alonee and Oliver came to the classroom door, they saw Ms. Amsterdam eating her lunch, a large salad. "Oh, we'll come later," Alonee offered.

"No, no," Ms. Amsterdam insisted, "come on in, you guys. You want one of these cherry tomatoes? They put the best cherry tomatoes in these salads."

"No thanks, "Oliver declined.

Ms. Amsterdam splashed some more ranch dressing on her salad. "I know I should use that vinegar stuff. But the ranch is sooo yummy," she said. "So, you guys have a problem? I'm all ears."

"Well," Oliver started, "this Princess of the Fair contest . . . it's sort of out of hand. Some of the kids are taking it way too seriously. They're doing ugly, mean things."

"Yeah," Alonee added, "like if you could change the rules or something, like having the teachers vote or something instead of the students. One pretty girl has gotten a bunch of glamour cards of herself printed up. They're all over the school. Now other kids are marking them up and . . . well . . ."

Ms. Amsterdam looked upset for a moment, but her happy smile quickly returned. She ate another forkful of salad and replied, "It's against the rules for anybody to be campaigning. A few students are going to cause problems. Most of the kids are doing fine. They are seriously pondering what girl most exhibits the qualities of kindness and compassion shown in Harriet Tubman. I think our kids will choose on the basis of inner beauty. Of course, our princess will be lovely too. All the girls at Tubman are lovely."

Oliver and Alonee exchanged a helpless look. As they left the classroom, photos of Neely Pelham swirled around their feet in the stiff afternoon breeze.

CHAPTER SIX

In the morning, Jasmine Benson was wearing a T-shirt bearing the likeness of a sad looking little girl. Beneath the child's tragic face were the words, "Fight Child Abuse and Neglect." Jasmine held in her hand a large coffee cup, also bearing the likeness of the forlorn child. Jasmine was standing beside the statue of Harriet Tubman. None of the students arriving for class could miss her.

"Hi Jasmine," Alonee said, "what's with the T-shirt and the coffee cup?"

"Oh, I'm collecting money to fight child abuse and neglect, Alonee," Jasmine replied. "A lot of that is going on, you know. People are sometimes mean to little children. And we have to do something about that. And they're neglected too. Sometimes parents leave them at home. And the children don't even have cereal to eat. I decided to do something about that."

"So," Alonee asked, "what organization are you collecting for?"

"Oh," Jasmine answered, "my mom told me to just collect the money. Then we'll find a worthy organization that helps children to give it to. I think some of those groups that help children are on the Internet. You know, Alonee, even teenagers can be abused. I worry about the children, don't you?" Jasmine had an earnest look on her face.

"Uh, yeah," Alonee agreed. "Jasmine, did you clear this with the office? I think before you do something like this, you have to tell them in the school office."

Oliver came walking up just then. He looked at Jasmine's T-shirt. "Oh, you belong to some organization that helps kids in trouble? What's the name of it?" he inquired.

Jaris arrived at about the same time and said, "Hey Jasmine, did somebody say it was all right for you to do this here? You know, collect money."

"I'm doing it for the children, for the poor little children," Jasmine responded with a soulful look.

Some students had told Mr. Hawthorne that a girl was collecting money by the Harriet Tubman statue. Now he came hurrying up, a perplexed look on his face. The vice principal looked at Jasmine. Then he asked, "Miss Benson, who gave you permission to be doing this?"

"I'm collecting money for the abused children," Jasmine answered. "I'm sure nobody is going to object to that." She smiled at Mr. Hawthorne. She said, "You're a kind man. I'm sure you're in favor of what I'm doing."

"Well," the vice principal replied, "it is very laudable that you are concerned for the children. But we must approve of the organizations that students solicit money for on campus. We have to follow procedure. We investigate the organization to make sure the money is going for the stated purpose. We cannot, you know, have students collecting money pell-mell. The money donated by generous students could be misused. It could be given to fraudulent organizations."

"I would never steal from the abused and neglected children," Jasmine stated solemnly.

"Of course you wouldn't," Mr. Hawthorne said.

Mr. Hawthorne tried to smile, but his face would not cooperate. He looked very upset by the whole situation. More students were gathering. Some were dropping bills into Jasmine's coffee cup.

"Miss Benson, would you come with me to the office. We'll get this all straightened out," Mr. Hawthorne requested. He waved his hands in the air. His fingers looked like the wings of blackbirds. "Girls, boys, no more money into the mug, please."

Marko Lane arrived then. "Hey look," he shouted. "That little crook Jasmine is over there collecting money for her own self. She's pretending it's for the poor children. She's got a scam going!"

"That's a lie," Jasmine screamed back at Marko. "I'm collecting for the abused children because I'm not heartless like you are, Marko Lane. Everybody knows you're so selfish you don't care about anybody but yourself. But *I* care about the downtrodden."

"Please!" Mr. Hawthorne commanded. "Let's go to the office, Miss Benson." He looked at the growing crowd of students. A girl was about to drop a five dollar bill into Jasmine's coffee cup. "No, no! No more money there," Mr. Hawthorne shouted.

Just at that moment, Mr. Pippin came toward them, lugging his battered briefcase. There were so many students on the sidewalk he couldn't get through. "What in heaven's name is going on now?" Mr. Pippin groaned.

"Mr. Pippin," Jasmine called out to the teacher. "You know me. I'm your student."

Mr. Pippin looked at the girl. She was a friend of Marko Lane's. That was enough to give Mr. Pippin the beginning of a stress headache. To himself he muttered, "Yes, Jasmine, I know you. Unfortunately. I wish I didn't know you. I wish I didn't know *any* of you!"

"Mr. Pippin," Jasmine pleaded, "tell Mr. Hawthorne that I really care about the abused and neglected children."

"*What* abused and neglected children?" Mr. Pippin cried. "Are there abused children around here? Who brought them? Call the police, for heavens sake."

"No, no!" Jasmine shouted to him, "I'm collecting money for them." Jasmine's voice had turned into a plaintive wail, "Mr. Hawthorne doesn't understand!"

Mr. Hawthorne began to look distraught. Mr. Pippin used his briefcase like a battering ram to clear a way for himself through the milling crowd. He just wanted to get to his classroom.

"Jaris," Mr. Hawthorne cried, "go to Ms. McDowell's classroom and tell her to come at once. Hurry over there, Jaris. Get her to come here!"

Jaris sprinted over to Ms. McDowell's classroom. "Ms. McDowell," he said to her, "Mr. Hawthorne is having a big problem over by Harriet Tubman's statue. He wants you to come quick!"

Ms. McDowell had a wild look on her face that Jaris had not seen before. "It's that princess thing isn't it?" she asked. "That stupid—!" Ms. McDowell hurried over to where the students were surging around Jasmine and Mr. Hawthorne. Destini Fletcher was digging into her purse for some money. Jasmine's coffee cup already had twenty dollars in it.

When Ms. McDowell arrived, Mr. Hawthorne reported hoarsely, "She's been collecting money for abused children without authorization. She won't come to the office with me, Ms. McDowell. We must get her to the office."

Ms. McDowell seized Jasmine's forearm firmly. "Come with me, Jasmine. We need to get to the office and straighten this out." Ms. McDowell confiscated the donation mug. Then she half led, half marched Jasmine toward the office, followed by a laughing crowd of students. Jasmine had burst into tears and was now sobbing loudly.

When all three reached the office, Ms. McDowell slammed the door behind them. Then she turned to Jasmine. "Stop crying and listen to me. No student is allowed to raise money for a charity without first getting permission from the school. What charity were you collecting for?"

"Uh, well," she began, between sobs, "Mom said just to collect. Then she'd find a good charity, maybe on the Internet."

Ms. McDowell sighed deeply. "Jasmine, that's unacceptable. I don't want you to be collecting money on this campus ever again.

Mr. Hawthorne doesn't want you to be collecting money."

"Correct," Mr. Hawthorne added, as he appeared in the doorway. "I certainly do not." He looked at Ms. McDowell with awe and admiration. Though he would never say so out loud, he was thinking that Ms. McDowell would be a better vice principal than he was. He peered from the window to see the crowd of students dispersing and going to their classrooms. The crisis had been resolved.

"We have some T-shirts from the lost and found, Jasmine," Ms. McDowell told her. "Pick one to wear for the rest of the day. We'll put the coffee cup right here with your T-shirt. You can collect them both after classes today. The money is being returned to the students who already donated. . . . Jasmine, stop crying. Do you hear me? There's no need to cry."

"I-I w-was just trying to help the children," Jasmine stammered. She took a red T-shirt to change into in the ladies room and left the office.

"What in the world is going on?" Ms. McDowell wondered aloud, glaring at Mr. Hawthorne. "How did we get into this mess? That awful Princess of the Fair contest strikes again. Correct me if I'm wrong. The girl who wins should exhibit compassion and kindness. Jasmine Benson? She hasn't been known to exhibit any such qualities. So now, as the voting draws near, she wants to establish her credentials as a caring human being!"

"Oh brother!" Mr. Hawthorne groaned.

"Do you remember, Bill," Ms. McDowell asked, "when Gayle brought up the idea of a fair with a princess who would be voted in by the kids? I opposed it, along with Mr. Pippin and a dozen other teachers. But the jellyheads prevailed."

"The jellyheads?" Mr. Hawthorne said.

"Never mind," Ms. McDowell snapped. "I have to return to my classroom and try to use what's left of the morning."

When Alonee, Jaris, Oliver, and Derrick got together for lunch, Jaris and Alonee told the others about the morning disaster. "Poor Mr. Hawthorne freaked," Jaris said. "There was Jasmine with her T-shirt and mug showing some sad looking kid, trying to collect money. And she didn't even have the name of an organization she planned to give the money to. They were gonna figure that out later."

"Jasmine is just trying so hard to win that contest," Alonee remarked. "She's afraid a lot of kids don't like her because she's selfish. Now she wants to prove she cares about the 'downtrodden,' as she calls them."

"I ran to get Ms. McDowell," Jaris added. "That is one cool lady to have in a crisis. She's the only one who got the chaos quieted down."

Derrick had been listening to the others and not saying anything. He looked deep in thought. Finally he said, "I saw something the other day that really blew my mind. You know Marko ditched Jasmine in a really big way, said a lot of awful stuff to her.

She wasn't expecting that. Anyway, Jasmine goes over to the grassy area right here. She flips herself down. She's crying and rolling around like she's dyin' or somethin'."

"Wow!" Jaris exclaimed. "She was that upset, huh?"

"Yeah," Derrick said. "Me and Destini came along and saw her. She looked terrible, like she was sick or somethin'. I felt like we should at least go see if she was okay, but Destini wouldn't. I don' blame Destini. Jasmine got her in trouble with her old boyfriend—Tyron. Destini got beat up by Tyron over that. Now Destini can't forgive Jasmine. So we just walked on by."

"Jasmine's been awfully mean and underhanded," Jaris remarked.

"Yeah," Alonee agreed. "I remember her doing that to Destini. She put Destini in danger."

Oliver said nothing. He just listened.

Derrick continued. "Lotta kids saw her there cryin' and thrashing around. Some of them laughed. Most of them just looked the other way. But then Sami Archer came along. I was pretty shocked by what happened, you guys."

"What went down, Derrick?" Oliver asked.

"Sami," Derrick went on, "she stops and stared over at Jasmine. She stands there for about a minute. Then she walks over to Jasmine. I didn't think I'd ever see something like that. Sami knelt down and put her arms around Jasmine and, you know, like comforted her. Sami did that."

"Man," Jaris remarked, "I think Jasmine's been meaner to Sami than she's been to anyone else, calling her ugly names. Remember when Jasmine insulted Sami's mom, and Sami slapped her down? Lucky we got that stopped before things went down too bad."

"I thought Sami really disliked Jasmine and for good reason," Alonee said.

"Yeah," Derrick said, nodding yes. "I just watched. Pretty soon Sami is holding Jasmine in her arms and bein' real nice.

And Sami helps Jasmine pick up her books 'cause she scattered them all over when she hit the grass. And Sami helps her up. And they go off together like old friends."

"I haven't known Sami Archer a long time like you guys," Oliver chimed in. "But she seems like a special person. The girl seems like the real deal."

"Yeah," Alonee agreed. "Sami won't ever lie to you. She'll tell you what you need to hear. And if you need a friend, they don't come any better than Sami."

Later in the day, Alonee ran into Neely Pelham. "I'm sorry about those pictures of me that got floated around," Neely apologized. "Marko went over the top there. I thought it was a bad idea right from the start."

"Well, they're all gone now," Alonee said. Neely was wearing a striking green top and black slacks. She looked even more stunning than usual. "So you and Marko dating now, huh?"

"Yeah, he's a lot of fun," Neely replied.

"You sure got together fast. One day he was with Jasmine and the next—" Alonee regretted those words the moment they escaped her lips. She had no right to be passing judgment on somebody's life. Her words sounded judgmental, so she quickly added, "I'm sorry. It's none of my business. But I was just kind of surprised."

"Yes, well," Neely admitted, "Marko has been flirting with me for a while. Anyway, Jasmine was really mean to Marko and he was hurting. So I was a shoulder to lean on and one thing led to another, I guess."

"Well, if you really like him, then it's good you got together," Alonee said, trying to make up for her mistake.

"Oh, we're not in love or anything," Neely confessed. "That takes time. It's just that we enjoy being together. And I really want to win this princess contest, and Marko's so supportive. He's like a little kid, all excited about me winning. Marko thinks he can do me a lot of good. There's a lot of pretty girls here at Tubman. I need all the help I can get."

Alonee didn't say anything more. But she put two and two together. Marko was using Neely to show Jasmine how quickly he could get another beautiful girlfriend. Neely was using Marko to help her get an edge in the contest. It wasn't love at first sight. It wasn't love at all. "They might not even *like* each other," Alonee thought.

As Alonee was leaving school, she saw Jasmine sitting on the small iron bench near Harriet Tubman's statue. Jasmine's mother always picked her up after school and drove her home. The girl wasn't crying, but she looked very sad.

"Hi Alonee," Jasmine said forlornly. "You know all about that mess this morning. I bet everybody's laughing at me over that."

"Yeah, I know what happened," Alonee admitted. "But nobody's laughing."

Sitting beside Jasmine on the bench was her coffee cup and her T-shirt, both depicting the poor little girl.

"Seem's like everything's going wrong for me," Jasmine groaned. "Like somebody put a curse on me. Maybe Marko did that. He's evil enough. I just wanted to prove to the school that I care about people too. I do, honest, Alonee. I woulda given the money to help kids in trouble. I never meant anything bad. Yeah, I was hoping that if I did something like that, everyone here at school would think I was a nice person. Maybe they'd vote for me for princess. I admit I was thinking that too."

"Well," Alonee responded, "everybody will forget about what happened."

Jasmine looked right at Alonee then. "I never could figure out why some of the kids here hate me, Alonee. Maybe I was blunt a few times. But I'm not a bad person. I think some of the girls hate me 'cause I'm beautiful and they're not. Girls are like that. They're real jealous. When I was a little girl at parties, all the grownups would gather around me. They would remark what a beautiful little girl I was. I was really pretty even then. I remember some of the other girls would come over and pinch me and stick out their tongues at me. It started way back then."

Jasmine paused a moment. Alonee felt she should say something to make Jasmine feel better. "When I was a kid, Mom would tell me I was no better than anybody else and no worse and that was that," Alonee said. "It really kept me on the ground."

Jasmine frowned deeply. "Marko, he's doing all he can to make Neely Pelham win. Like those pictures of her he spread around. Don't even look like her. She really wants to win. She's like crazy to win. She's thinking about this contest twenty-four hours a day. She's not a nice person. She's selfish and cold. She's not interested in helping other people at all. I'd rather see some dog like Ryann Kern win that contest instead of Neely. I just want Neely to lose so bad."

"Jasmine," Alonee scolded, "don't call Ryann a dog. That's the kind of thing Marko does. And don't go overboard on wanting to win the contest. It's just a stupid Princess of the Fair deal at a little high school. It's not the preliminaries for Miss Universe."

"I know," Jasmine admitted. "But I've never won any beauty contests, not even little ones. And I'm beautiful enough to win. I was such a beautiful little girl that I could have started wining pageants and building up a resume. But my parents are so protective that they stifled me. They were afraid somebody would see my pictures and kidnap me! My parents were so *selfish*!"

"No," Alonee said. "They just loved you, Jasmine."

"You know what *I* wish," Jasmine said.

"No," Alonee replied, afraid to ask.

"I wish," Jasmine began, "that Neely Pelham's face would break out in the worst case of acne the world has ever seen. I wish her entire face would be a mass of red, ugly pimples! I wish she would look so ugly that kids would look at her and run screaming away. I wish she'd get a big pimple right at the end of her pert little nose. And I wish it would be the size of a golf ball."

"Jasmine, for just a few seconds," Alonee said, "I thought maybe you had changed a little. I thought breaking up with Marko had opened your eyes about people being cruel to each other. I thought maybe you were really trying to be a nicer, better person. But what you just said is mean and spiteful. And it makes me really sad."

"Oh, don't be such a bleeding heart, Alonee Lennox," Jasmine protested. "You're so sappy it makes me sick. I'm honest enough to admit how I feel. People like you pretend they're all nice and noble. And deep down in your heart you want bad things to happen to people you hate too."

"I don't hate anybody," Alonee said.

"Come on, Alonee. If you wanted something as bad as I want to be princess, you'd do anything to get it too," Jasmine told her.

"Maybe," Alonee admitted. "But I hope if I ever want something so bad that I'm wishing hurt on other people, I hope I don't get what I want. And I hope that life slaps me down so hard it takes my breath away."

"You're crazy," Jasmine snapped. "You're just crazy." Jasmine saw her father pull into the parking lot. She picked up her T-shirt and coffee mug and said, "There's that selfish man who wouldn't let me be in beauty pageants. I hope he knows someday that he ruined my life."

Alonee watched Jasmine run to her father's car. In the driver's seat, she caught sight of a weary-looking businessman sitting at the wheel. And she felt very sorry for him.

CHAPTER SEVEN

As Alonee was walking home, Sami caught up to her. Alonee hated what she was thinking right now. Sami was a fool to reach out to Jasmine as she did. Jasmine was a lost cause. She was too mean and selfish to deserve any sympathy. Sami was just wasting her big heart on a cold stone. But Alonee didn't want thoughts like that in her head. Her parents had brought her up to be a bigger person than that. Everybody was worth saving, they taught Alonee. Everyone had a seed of goodness in their soul. It was everyone's duty to feed and water that seed.

"Hi Alonee," Sami called. "Boy, Mr. Goodman really loaded on the math homework, didn't he? I got me so much homework it's gonna take me half the night."

"Yeah," Alonee agreed, "he sure did give a lot."

The girls walked on. Then Alonee said, "Derrick told us at lunch today that you tried to help Jasmine the other day. You know, when she was crying under the eucalyptus trees."

"Derrick got a big mouth," Sami replied. "He's a good boy. Just sometime he talk too much."

"It was really good of you to try to help her," Alonee told her. "Wow, Sami, she's been so mean to all of us, especially you."

"I didn't do nothin' but looked to see if she was okay," Sami explained. "I helped her pick up her books. She threw them all over. I was worried she might be really sick or something. Couldn't just let her lay there howlin'."

"I really admire you, Sami," Alonee said. "You're able to forgive. I'm not sure I could."

"Nothin' to forgive," Sami objected. "She got a dirty mouth and a mean streak runnin' pretty deep. But a time like that, you don't think about that stuff. Somebody hurtin' bad and you gotta do something. It's what we're here for, girl."

"You sound like Pastor Bromley," Alone commented, smiling.

"No way!" Sami protested. "I ain' no preacher. But if we on this earth, we gotta be there for each other. You hear what I'm sayin'? Like if you see a car crash and somebody trapped in there. You don't look in and say, 'Hey dude, you been good this year? 'Cause if you have, I'll help you out. But if you be one of those no-goods, you just stay in that old wrecked car and die.' "

"Yeah," was all Alonee could say.

"Like herself," Sami went on, pointing to the statue of Harriet Tubman, "standing there in front of the school, Alonee. In the dark of the night when she sang out for her fellow slaves to join her in the run for freedom. You think she asked them if they were sinners or not? Some of them likely were chicken thieves. Maybe somebody cheated on his woman. Harriet Tubman didn't look into that. She just called them out to run with her to freedom land, no matter who they were."

"Yes," Alonee said and found herself nodding yes.

"Or when Harriet Tubman worked in that army hospital in Fernandina, Florida," Sami continued. "Cared for those boys sufferin' smallpox. She cooled all their heads, the good and the bad. She work day and night to save those boys. Likely some were lots worse than Jasmine Benson. Harriet saw hurt and went in and took care of those boys. She risked her life. I done nothin', Alonee. I patted a girl on the back, when she was cryin' her eyes out. That was nothin'. You tell that boy Derrick to keep his mouth shut. That boy talks too much. He makin' a mountain out of a molehill. He a sweet boy. But he got too big a mouth."

"I'm glad you're my friend, Sami," Alonee said.

"Well, I'm glad you're my friend too, Alonee," Sami replied. "How's it goin' with that Oliver boy? Now *there's* a sweet boy. He put in hours helping that Eric Carney bring up his science grade. He saved that boy."

"I like him a lot, Sami," Alonee said. "You know I always had a crush on Jaris. I guess you knew. I never came right out and told anybody but . . ."

Sami laughed. "You having that thing for Jaris was like the elephant in the livin' room, Alonee. Everybody saw it but nobody want to talk about it."

"Well, I kept that crush going for a long time," Alonee chuckled. "Too long. I still have a soft spot in my heart for Jaris. I guess I always will. But I don't think about him all the time like I used to. I think about Oliver!"

Sami gave Alonee a big hug. "I am so glad for you, girl. I am so glad for you I could just burst out singing!" Sami said.

"You still hang out a lot with Matson Malloy, huh?" Alonee asked. Matson had been a shy foster child until he took up track at Tubman. Now he was blossoming.

"Yeah, we have fun together," Sami replied. "I get to all the track meets. I yell my head off for Matson, especially when he beats the pants off of Marko! Coach Curry is sayin' his best track stars are Kevin Walker and Matson. They leave old Marko in the dust wonderin' what just went by."

With that, Sami turned off toward her house, calling good-bye over her shoulder.

When Alonee got to her house, Mom was in the kitchen making a salad for dinner.

"Mom, something I wanted to talk to you about," Alonee announced. "Sereeta's mother is having a birthday soon. She's gonna be thirty-six or something. Lately, things have been pretty cold between Sereeta and her mom. I know it's bothering Sereeta a lot. But she won't talk about it. They're having a party for Sereeta's mother at the house on a Friday night. But Sereeta's stepdad sort of doesn't want Sereeta there."

Alonee's mother frowned. "You mean Sereeta isn't welcome to her own mother's birthday party?" she asked indignantly.

"Well, Perry, the stepfather," Alonee explained, "he didn't come right out and tell Sereeta she shouldn't come. But he said the karma wasn't right."

"The *karma*? I'd like to whack him over the head with his karma," Mom snapped.

"He told Sereeta it was going to be an adult party with drinks and stuff, and she'd feel awkward. So, anyway, he suggested Sereeta give her own party for her mother on Sunday of that week. Sereeta liked that idea. We thought Jaris's mom and Sami's mom and you and Sereeta's friends could get something together that'd be real nice and . . ." Alonee smiled at her mother in the way she smiled when she wanted something important.

Mom grinned. "You guys want the party here, right?"

"Well," Alonee wheedled, "Sami's mom said she'd bring the cake. Jaris's mom would bring salad and fruit. So all we'd have to worry about is maybe a casserole."

"I'd fry chicken," Alonee's mother declared. "What's a down-home party without fried chicken? Of course, I'd love to have the party here for Sereeta's mom. She and I and Monie and Mattie were good friends in the old days. We could do it out on the patio and decorate real nice."

Alonee gave her mother a hug. "Oh, thanks Mom! It'll mean so much to Sereeta."

"I got along fine with Olivia when she was married to Tom," Alonee's mother re-marked. "We had a lot of fun together. We'd all go to get our hair done at the same little salon—me, Mattie Archer, Monie Spain, and Olivia. We'd giggle like teenagers."

"Well," Alonee explained, "since Sereeta moved in with her grandmother, she hasn't had much to do with her mom. And I know it's hard on her. This'll be so great."

"I think it's a wonderful idea, even if that old karma guy first suggested it," Mom laughed.

"Mom," Alonee added, "on Saturday me and Sereeta and Sami are going shopping. Sereeta is going to find a special birthday gift for her mother. Even though they've, you know, had problems, Sereeta really loves her mom."

"And I'm sure her mother loves Sereeta as best she can," Alonee's mother said.

On Saturday morning, the three girls caught a bus to the best mall in the area. At the mall, they started their hunt for the best gift.

"Mom always hated birthdays," Sereeta remarked, "because they remind her that she's getting older. So I have to get her something young and frivolous. That's so she remembers she's not over the hill yet."

"She like jewelry?" Sami asked.

"Yeah," Sereeta responded, "but Perry is getting her something fabulous. He's giving her a diamond necklace."

"They getting along better now?" Sami asked.

"I guess," Sereeta answered, a little sadly. "I don't really know. Perry told me about the diamond necklace when he called telling me about their party. I call my mom a lot. But we don't talk long. She sort of doesn't seem to have anything to say. I told her about the Princess of the Fair contest, and she said she hoped I'd win. But then I told her I didn't want to, and she just said 'Oh.' Then she said she wished she were young enough to be in beauty pageants and stuff."

"Look," Alonee pointed. "These are fabulous tops—and they're marked down. I've seen your mom wearing stuff like this, Sereeta. She's a small, right?"

"Oh yeah!" Sereeta said. "And these are her kind of tops all right. Wow, look at this yellow and orange one! Isn't it beautiful? Mom would love this. They got it in small?" Sereeta began going wildly through the rack. "Large . . . large . . . extra large . . ." She recited the sizes.

"Small!" Alonee cried. "Here's one in small! Yesss!"

"How much is it?" Sereeta asked, getting out her wallet.

"Girl," Sami cried, "it's twenty-seven dollars, and it's marked down from fifty-two dollars!"

"I'll take it," Sereeta said, heading for the cash register with the top. Sereeta had been working at the frozen yogurt shop for several months. She had been saving a lot of money for special occasions like this. Sereeta's mother and stepfather paid Sereeta's grandma for room and board. But still Grandma was living mainly on her Social Security check. She didn't have much left over each month.

The girls headed for the food court for fish tacos and soda. "Sereeta," Sami asked, "does your mom and grandma talk very often?"

"No," Sereeta admitted. "She's my dad's mother, you know. When my parents got their divorce, grandma sort of blamed Mom and let Mom know it. They've had hard feelings ever since. I think that's one of the reasons why Mom has turned kinda cold to me since I moved there."

"Yeah," Alonee said, "but your mother and stepfather wanted you to go to boarding school for your senior year. That was so lame."

"Yeah," Sereeta agreed. Her fish taco was just sitting there as she sipped her cola.

"Eat up, girl," Sami urged her. "You skinny enough as it is."

Sereeta smiled and started nibbling on the taco.

"It's going to be a nice party at my house next Sunday," Alonee commented. "My mom's really excited. She and your mom used to be pretty close, Sereeta."

"My mama's gonna make one of her famous cakes," Sami declared. "Mama's cakes are world famous. We know that 'cause one time she entered one of her cakes in a contest and she won a thousand dollars. What kinda cake your mom like, Sereeta?"

"She's always liked chocolate," Sereeta replied. "The more chocolaty the better."

"Okay. We'll do chocolate frosting too," Sami decided. "What should Mama write on the top?"

"Don't mention birthday," Sereeta thought. "How about "Love, Sereeta.' Nice and simple."

"Cool," Sami said.

After they finished lunch, the girls went to the card shop. They bought wrapping paper and ribbon. Then they searched for the right birthday card.

"Look at all the cards from daughter to mom," Sereeta noted, beginning to open them and read the messages. The words were all about the same. They said things like "To Mom, you were always there for me" and "To Mom, my biggest supporter and most faithful fan." Sereeta began to look frustrated as she searched for the right card.

The beautiful sentiments didn't apply to Sereeta's relationship with her mother. Since her mom remarried, the mother-daughter bond had weakened seriously. Sereeta felt ignored.

"Hey, I got just the one," Sami announced, holding up a beautiful card. It read, "To Mom, you make all my friends' moms jealous 'cause you're so beautiful!" It ended with a simple, "Love," and the daughter just had to write her name.

Sereeta smiled and nodded, "Yes, she'll like that." Mercifully, it said nothing about all Olivia Manley had meant in her daughter's life, the support, the love, the being there.

The girls all ended up at Sereeta's grandmother's house, where they wrapped the gift.

Sereeta's grandmother was almost seventy, and she had a few health problems. She had arthritis in her knees and high blood pressure. The doctor was always changing the medication and causing more problems. Still in all, she was in pretty good shape. She took long walks and was trim and fit.

"Look, Grandma, isn't this a pretty top?" Sereeta held up the garment.

Sereeta's grandmother smiled and nodded. "Looks perfect for your mother, sweetheart. Livy always liked bright colors." Grandma did not like her former daughter-in-law, and Sereeta knew that. But Grandma was a noble enough person not to let her feelings show. She never criticized Sereeta's mother to Sereeta. She understood the pain her granddaughter was going through. She didn't want to add to it by introducing another level of bitterness. That was another reason Sereeta had for loving her grandmother.

The girls giggled as they made several false starts in wrapping the package. Finally, they got it right with a little help from Grandma. They ended up with a beautifully wrapped gift.

"I don't think she expects me to give her a gift," Sereeta remarked. "She'll be really surprised that I got her this. I think she'll be touched. I mean, I know she feels bad that Perry kinda dis-invited me to the party on Friday night. So she's gonna think

I'm ticked off, and that's why this gift is gonna be a big shock."

"You already sent her an invitation to the party on Sunday, Sereeta?" Alonee asked.

"Oh yeah, Alonee," Sereeta replied. "The minute you called me that night and said your mom was cool with having it at your house. I emailed Mom. I told her the party was at one at the Lennox house. I told her her friends and mine were coming, and it was gonna be great fun. I told her we were all looking forward to celebrating her birthday. I said Mattie and Dawna and Monie were really excited about getting the old gang together again."

"She email you back yet?" Sami asked.

"Oh no," Sereeta responded. "She usually doesn't answer her email. But she reads it. And just in case, I sent another invitation by regular mail. So we can't miss."

A few minutes later, Alonee and Sami caught the bus at the end of the street to go home. They stood there waiting for people to get off the bus so they could get on.

Sami asked, "Alonee, you think she's gonna come, don't you?"

"I can't believe she wouldn't," Alonee replied with a shudder.

Sami had a strange look on her face. "Girl, I got a bad feeling about this. I'm probably all wrong and I hope to heaven I am. But I got this bad feeling."

They found seats in the middle of the bus, and it rolled toward their stops.

"I don't even want to think about that," Alonee asserted.

"I hear what you're sayin' girl," Sami agreed in a heavy voice.

CHAPTER EIGHT

Sereeta's birthday party for her mother was a whole week away. But Alonee was surprised at how excited Sereeta was already getting. It was as if Sereeta had been hungering for a long time for this opportunity to reconnect with her mother. She had found a peaceful haven with her beloved grandmother. But she couldn't help missing her mom.

Alonee remembered that at one time Sereeta had wept bitterly about her relationship with her mother. Jaris had told Alonee about it. "If only I'd stop wanting her to be a mother," Sereeta had complained at the time. "I could always tell she wasn't crazy about me. I mean, like, you know, some mothers are. Why can't I just stop wanting what I'll never have?"

During the week before the party, everybody noticed Sereeta's upbeat spirit.

"Hey girl, you look radiant," Matson Malloy noted. "Is it about the Princess of the Fair contest?"

"No," Sereeta laughed. "I'm planning a birthday party for my mom. I think it's gonna be so good and I can't wait. It's gonna bring me and my mother closer, I think."

Alonee noticed Sereeta's high spirits too and said so to her. Sereeta then confided that the birthday party was coming at just the right time. "Mom and Perry hired a nanny. Little Jake was causing them a lot of stress. That might have been part of the tension at home. I mean, Perry resented all the time Mom was spending with Jake. And she was neglecting Perry. Now they're going to parties again. Perry likes that. When Perry's happy, Mom's happy. I think Mom stopped drinking so much too.

She was drowning her sorrows. Now she hasn't got that many sorrows. So it's a real good time for Mom and me to patch things up too. And what makes it so special, her old girlfriends will be there. Things'll be warm and comfortable for her."

As Alonee and Sereeta were talking, Jasmine came along. "Hey Sereeta," Jasmine commented. "You look happy. You thinkin' you're gonna win the contest, right?"

Sereeta laughed, "I've forgotten about that stupid thing, Jasmine."

"Get real," Jasmine told her. "Some boys are taking polls. You know, rating the chicks with the best chance. You want to hear the latest buzz?"

"Not really," Sereeta replied.

Jasmine ignored her and started telling them what she'd heard. "Lissen up, girls. Everette is in the know. He's talking to a lot of dudes. Been some big changes from the last poll. I'll just give you the top five. Number five is Carissa Polson. She's dropped from number four. Neely Pelham is now four.

She's gone way up. She's on the move. Three has stayed the same. Alonee, you're still there. I'm two. Sereeta, you're number one. But Everette tells me I'm closing the gap, girl. And I still got a few tricks up my sleeve."

"Everette Keenan is such a jerk," Alonee remarked. "Doesn't he have anything better to do than run these silly polls?"

Jasmine ignored Alonee and turned to Sereeta. "Girl, we both gotta worry about Neely Pelham. She could overtake the both of us in the final laps."

"Neely Pelham on the outside, coming on strong," Alonee announced, imitating the voice of a racetrack announcer. "Jasmine and Sereeta, neck in neck. But here comes Neely. She's putting on a last-minute surge. *There she goes!*"

Sereeta doubled over laughing.

On Friday night, the guests began arriving early for the party at the house where Sereeta used to live with her parents. Most of the well dressed couples streaming into the house were business friends of Perry Manley. He was eager to show off his beautiful wife.

Also on that night, Sereeta got a call from Viola Thorne. The Thorne family lived next door to the Manleys, and Viola was a year younger than Sereeta. The girls used to be casual friends. Viola commented on the phone, "I thought you'd be over here for the party, Sereeta. I mean, you're her daughter. Why aren't you here?"

"Well, I don't fit in with my stepfather's friends," Sereeta explained. "It would be awkward for me to be there. I'm having my own party for my mom on Sunday. Some of mom's old friends and my friends."

"Oh," Viola said. "Well, you should hear the music pouring out of there. Horrible disco. People are laughing and hollering. My mom's mad. She says they're making too much noise already. If it goes on into the night, she's gonna call the police. . . . Sereeta, I'm looking out my window. Your mom's on the porch greeting some people.

She's wearing a gold lamé dress! It's so short. It's off the shoulders too. She looks like a kid, Sereeta!"

They talked for a while, then Viola hung up. Sereeta thought to herself that this was what Mom wanted more than anything. She wanted to look young, to feel young, to dress young, to surround herself with youth. She couldn't be young again. But she could pretend for a while.

Sereeta called Alonee and told her about the party. "Looks like Mom is having a ball," Sereeta told her.

"I bet your mom'll have more fun at our party, Sereeta," Alonee said.

"Yeah," Sereeta agreed. They spoke a little longer and then ended the call.

Her mother and stepfather had not invited any of the couples she and her first husband had socialized with—the Spains, the Lennoxes, the Archers. Perry wouldn't have wanted anybody there who remembered when his wife was married to someone else.

Sereeta lay down on her bed in her grandmother's house. She looked at the beautifully wrapped gift in the chair across the room. Sereeta tried to imagine the big smile breaking out on her mother's face. Mom would be so surprised.

"Oh sweetie," Mom would say when she opened the box. "This is so beautiful. I never dreamed . . . oh sweetie, how thoughtful of you. I do love you so, Sereeta. I miss you. You have to come over to the house more. We have to do some of the things we used to do. Go down to the bay and watch the seagulls. Remember when you were a little girl and you'd laugh at the pelicans?"

And then they would hug. Sereeta's mother always wore a wonderful perfume. And she wouldn't tell anybody what it was. Whenever Sereeta would hug her mother, the incredible aroma would wash over her. Sereeta tried to imagine what it would be like in her mother's arms, overcome by sweetness again. It would be like being enveloped in a mother's love.

The next Sunday morning, Alonee and Sami began work on the birthday party decorations. They had just returned from singing in the praise choir at Pastor Bromley's church. In the backyard, they tied balloons from tree branches and from the roof of the gazebo.

Inside the Lennox house, by quarter to twelve, the aroma of fried chicken filled the air. Monie Spain had arrived with a beautiful Asian salad that her husband, Lorenzo, had put together. Dawna Lennox put out watermelon and cantaloupe in cocktail glasses. There was sparkling apple cider to drink. The chocolate cake was in another room, waiting for its grand entrance. "My, don't it look nice!" Mattie Archer cried.

The three lady friends of Sereeta's mother each brought a small gift. Mattie had a little cut glass candy dish. Monie brought a glass figurine of a dancing girl. She remembered how Olivia had collected those. Dawna brought a leather manicure set.

The gifts all sat on a table, dominated by the large box from Sereeta.

As the one o'clock hour drew near, Alonee grew tense. She glanced frequently at Sereeta's happy, excited face, which lit up everytime a car turned down the street. Olivia Manley drove a maroon Honda Accord. Sereeta had seen it around town several times. But she never rode in it.

Sereeta moved closer to the window in order to spot her mother's car at the earliest possible moment. The plan was for everyone to shout "Happy birthday!" as Sereeta's mother came in.

At one o'clock, Sami leaned close to Alonee. She whispered, "Girl, I am gonna die. What is goin' on?"

There was mild, good-natured worry among the mothers. Monica Spain joked that Olivia was always late and that she would be late for her own funeral. There was a smattering of nervous laughter. Mattie Archer said she'd better come quick, or they were going to eat all the fried chicken. Nobody laughed.

Sereeta's smile grew frayed at the edges. Something entered her eyes, at first like a small, timid animal creeping in. But slowly it became more frightening.

Alonee's mother suggested, "Well, why don't I just call over there and see what the hang-up is. Could be car trouble or something."

"Yes," Monica agreed. "Those things happen at the most inopportune times."

Sami looked at Alonee. Sami grabbed Alonee's hand and held on tight. Sami was suffering intensely because of the effect on Sereeta if the worst were to happen.

What if Olivia Manley never came?

The room, filled with chattering, grew quiet.

"Hi," Alonee's mother said. "This is Dawna Lennox and I'd like to speak to Olivia Manley." Apparently, Mrs. Lennox was talking to the nanny at the Manley house. "Oh. Well, is Mr. Manley in? . . . Yes, please."

Alonee didn't want to look at Sereeta. But she did anyway. Sereeta stood there

143

frozen, like a statue. There was no expression on her face.

"Hello, Mr. Manley," Alonee's mom began. "This is Dawna Lennox, one of Olivia's friends. Sereeta and some of her friends are having a birthday party for Olivia, here at my house. Sereeta emailed her about it about a week ago. . . . Oh, she did? I see. I'm sorry to hear that. . . . I see. All right then . . . ." She put down the phone.

Alonee felt sorry for her mother.

"Mr. Manley said your mother's not feeling well, Sereeta," Mrs. Lennox said. "He said she'd eaten something that didn't agree with her. He said he was sorry. He hoped everyone understood."

"He say why he didn't call before and say she wasn't coming?" Mattie Archer asked in a harsh voice.

"No," Alonee's mother replied. She turned to Sereeta and said, "I'm sorry, honey. I'm really sorry."

There was a mild smile on Sereeta's face. "Well, I guess the party's off then!"

She rushed out and began destroying the balloons. The pop-pop sounds filled the air like gunfire.

Alonee ran outside too and tried to reach Sereeta. But Sereeta darted away. Sami came out then. She spoke in a businesslike voice that had a strange, calming effect on Sereeta. "Com'n, we got work to do. We're gonna load up Mom's van. Put all the food in there. Come on Sereeta, you carry the Asian salad. And be sure you put the aluminum wrap on top. We're takin' the chicken and the cake and the fruit. We goin' to Grandma's house. We gotta get there before the chicken gets cold."

Sereeta stood there for a moment. Sami took her hand firmly and spoke to her. "Grandma goin' to be glad to see all this good food, girl. Know what, Sereeta? We never got much chance to socialize with your grandma. Now's the time."

They all piled into the van with the food. They held the food dishes firmly on their laps as Mattie Archer drove the short distance to Grandma's house. They pulled into the driveway as Bessie Prince came out the front door. She stared at the van and at the mothers and girls piling out. Sami was out first, "Hi, Mrs. Prince!" she hailed. "We all friends of Sereeta. Her mom got sick and couldn't come to the birthday party. So we bringin' the party here. We gonna celebrate wherever you say."

Bessie Prince smiled and responded. "Well Lordy, come on in!" She helped to carry in the food, all the while saying, "Land sakes, how good it all looks!"

When they were all seated around the table and the food was ready to eat, Bessie Prince said grace. "Well, thanks to the Lord for all this. I'd like to celebrate the day my mama and papa brought us all to California from Mississippi. That was a glory day for sure." She reached over and took Sereeta's hand. Everybody else joined hands too. "Thank you, Lord, for good friends. And for my granddaughter who is precious to me.

And for the fried chicken and the salad and the big cake."

Monica Spain had met Bessie Prince when Olivia and Tom were married. But she never knew her well. Now Bessie Prince regaled them all with stories of her life in Mississippi. She told them how her parents drove to California in an old Plymouth after World War II. She described how they blew tires in the desert heat and were often stranded. "We drove the Mother Road, Route 66," she recollected, her eyes moistening. "And I met my husband, a skinny black boy. We had a son and named him Tom. That's your daddy, Sereeta."

As Grandma entertained everyone with her stories, Alonee and Sami noticed a change in Sereeta. When it had become obvious that Sereeta's mother was not coming to the party, Sereeta had started coming unglued. Alonee and Sami had been worried. But when Mattie Archer herded everybody into the van with Sami's help, Sereeta started to change. Her sorrow turned to a kind of resignation. Now, finally, it was one of acceptance. She smiled at her grandmother's stories. She even laughed when Grandma told about the desert tarantula that got into the car as they were crossing the hot sands.

Before long they'd all eaten. The leftovers were in the refrigerator and freezer. Bessie Prince couldn't have thanked her unexpected guests more. "You're all angels," she declared, hugging everybody. Sami put her arms around Bessie Prince and announced, "Sereeta, you got the greatest grandma in the world."

Alonee hugged Sereeta. So did Sami and the mothers. Sereeta cried a little, but the tears weren't bitter anymore. She even smiled a little as the van pulled away from the house.

Inside the van, Mattie turned to her daughter. "That was a great idea, Sami," she said. "We turned a disaster into a blessing."

"Well, we had to do somethin'," Sami asserted. "Her mom not coming was a big kick in the teeth."

"Do you think Olivia was really sick?" Alonee's mother asked.

Monica Spain shook her head sadly. "The kind of sick that comes out of a bottle. She probably totally forgot about the party."

Mattie Archer dropped everyone by their cars at the Lennox house. When everyone was gone, Alonee went into the house with her mother. She glanced into the backyard at the ruined decorations. Then, inside, she looked at the wrapped gifts, unopened.

"What about these?" Alonee asked.

"We'll return them," her mother replied. "You can take Sereeta's gift to school. She can do what she wants with it"

"Oh Mom," Alonee sighed. "You should have seen how happy Sereeta was when she picked out that gift for her mom. She was just bubbling over."

Mom frowned. "Honey, it just beats me how these things happen. We all—Monie, Mattie, Livy, and I—started out our married lives with men we loved. We were blessed with children we loved. I still love your father, and you kids are precious to me. I know Monie and Mattie feel the same way. But with Livy, something went wrong. I don't know how to explain it. Thank God for Sami, Alonee. That girl has a special touch, a way to heal. Sereeta was in terrible shape. Sami got her calmed down and caught up in the crazy idea of going over to Grandma's house. It was just the right thing. It was balm to her soul. Sami, she's one of the special ones."

"Yeah, Mom," Alonee agreed, thoughtfully.

CHAPTER NINE

Jasmine Benson was standing in front of Harriet Tubman's statue on Monday with a large basket of flowers. She was handing each arriving student a yellow daisy and saying, "Peace and love from Jasmine Benson."

"What's this?" a boy asked. "You selling daisies for a good cause now, Jasmine?"

"I'm not selling anything," Jasmine replied in a dreamy voice. "I'm wishing everybody peace and love. I think that's what the world needs now."

When Alonee and Sami came along, Jasmine didn't offer them daisies. She knew they wouldn't vote for her. She didn't want to waste her flowers on them.

Alonee and Sami stood there for a few minutes, watching Jasmine passing out the daisies.

"She thinks giving out a yellow daisy is going to win her some votes?" Alonee wondered.

"Could work," Sami laughed. "Mosta the kids don't give a hoot about this contest anyways. Votin' for somebody who give them a daisy is about as good a reason as any. All most of us want from the fair is eatin' some good food and havin' some fun. Don' matter what chick is walking around with a tiara on her head."

Most of the students were dropping their daisies on the sidewalk as they went to class, causing a considerable mess. Isaac, the maintenance man, noted that the trail of daisies led to the girl with the basket who stood by Harriet Tubman's statue.

"Hey there, missy," Isaac shouted, "what're you up to here?"

"Oh," Jasmine responded, "I'm just passing out daisies and wishing peace and love to everyone."

Isaac cut her off. "Girl, I'm all for peace and love. But I don't 'ppreciate having to clean up piles of dead flowers on the walk-ways."

"They're not dead," Jasmine said. "I just bought them at the little corner store. They're lovely living daisies."

"They pretty much dead," Isaac objected, "after they're in some kid's sweaty hand for a few minutes. You figure a kid's going to carry the flower around all day? No, she gonna drop it on my walkways. And guess who has to sweep 'em all up. Now quit it, girl."

Jasmine had a large number of daisies left in her basket. But she moved away from the Harriet Tubman statue. She carried her basket toward her first class— English. Usually Jasmine sat in the middle of the classroom. Today she sat way in the back with her basket.

When Marko and his friends came in, they saw the basket of daisies. One of the boys remarked, "Hey Marko, your old girl-friend got a basket of daisies. They from you?" Marko didn't enjoy being the butt of jokes, even from his friends. He glared at Jasmine.

As other students arrived, Jasmine quickly passed them daisies, whispering, "Peace and love from Jasmine Benson." Most of the students looked at the flowers in a puzzled way and dropped them on the floor. By the time Mr. Pippin arrived, the floor was littered with daisies. Some had already been stepped on, creating a worse mess.

Mr. Pippin came in and took a double take at the floor. "What's all over the floor?" he demanded.

"Flowers," Marko said. "That crazy chick in the back, Jasmine Benson, she's passing them out so she gets more votes to be Princess of the Fair."

Mr. Pippin frowned. "We do not use derogatory slurs against people, Marko."

Then he stared at Jasmine. "Are you passing out flowers in my classroom?" he asked.

"I'm using them as symbols of peace and love," Jasmine replied. "I'm sure you're in favor of peace and love, Mr. Pippin."

"Good grief!" Mr. Pippin groaned. "What will they think of next? Jasmine, cease and desist at once! Oliver, Marko, collect every one of these flowers on the floor and put them in the trash."

As Marko was gathering daisies from the floor near Jasmine's desk, he whispered to her. "Well, at least you can count on the litterbug vote."

When Oliver carried the trash can filled with wilted daisies to the front, he could barely keep from laughing. Only Mr. Pippin's outraged look sobered him. . . .

"Today we shall discuss clichés as they appear in nonfiction," Mr. Pippin began. "For example, one might say 'Life is difficult,' or use the cliché 'Life is no bed of roses.' The overused cliché makes the language stale and unappealing. Can anyone offer more examples?"

Alonee answered, "When a race is close, they might call it 'nip and tuck.'"

Marko offered, "When somebody does something real stupid, you'd say that person is 'dumb as an ox.' Like when they throw flowers all over the floor in a lame try at winning a contest."

"Marko," Mr. Pippin scolded, "we do not wish to turn this discussion into personal attacks on other people. Understand?"

"Clear as a bell, Mr. Pippin," Marko replied.

"Has anyone else an example of a cliché?" Mr. Pippin asked.

"When you're too dumb to even know what you're doing is stupid, you're 'blind as a bat,'" Marko suggested. Mr. Pippin dropped his head and shook it.

After class, Jasmine carried her basket of daisies out with her. Mr. Pippin pursued her. He asked, "Jasmine, what do you intend to do with the rest of the flowers?"

"I thought I'd, you know, pass them out," Jasmine said.

"Please, Jasmine, most of them are dead," Mr. Pippin requested. "They've been out of water for a long time. Let's put them in the trash now."

Jasmine looked in her basket. True, the daisies didn't look as fresh as they did early this morning when she bought them. But they looked okay. "Mr. Pippin, I paid good money for these daisies. Maybe I'll pour some water on them to revive them."

"The chick is crazy as a loon," Marko commented from several yards away, to the wild laugher of his friends. Just then, Ms. Amsterdam came walking along. She stared in wonderment at the strange sight of Jasmine and Mr. Pippin. They were grasping opposite ends of the daisy basket. Each was tugging to get it away from the other. She drew closer and inquired, "May I be of help?"

"Ah!" Mr. Pippin said savagely. "The brains behind this lovely Princess of the

Fair scheme. Congratulations, Ms. Amsterdam, on your cleverness. The would-be princesses are whipping themselves into a frenzy in an effort to win. This girl here has been throwing dead flowers all over the school to win friends and votes."

"I was just passing out daisies in the name of peace and love," Jasmine whispered.

"Now, now dear," Ms. Amsterdam said soothingly, "we mustn't throw flowers on Mr. Pippin's floor."

"I d-didn't," Jasmine stammered. "I was just—"

"Ms. Amsterdam," Mr. Pippin interrupted, "in the name of common decency, will you take charge of this overwrought girl and her flower basket? Please get them both out of my sight." Beads of perspiration popped out on his brow.

"Oh man," Marko remarked, "that crazy chick is gonna lose in the competition for sure. They better start fitting Neely for the tiara."

Ms. Amsterdam seized the basket and grasped Jasmine's hand. "Come along, dear," she said. "Wilted flowers make wonderful mulch. Won't that be nice? Your little daisies will help other plants to flourish."

At the end of the school day, when Alonee's father came to pick her up, he had the birthday present Sereeta had planned to give her mother. Alonee took it from him, planning to give it to Sereeta. But Sereeta came running over to the car. "Thanks, Mr. Lennox," she said, taking the package.

"I'm really sorry your mom got sick and missed the party, Sereeta," Alonee's father told her.

"Thanks," Sereeta replied. She carried the box away toward the school. Alonee watched her for a few minutes, then she said, "Dad, would you wait here about ten minutes? I want to make sure Sereeta's okay."

"Sure honey," her father agreed. "Take your time."

Alonee trailed Sereeta at a distance. Sereeta seemed fine all day in class.

Now she looked troubled. Sereeta looked so underweight and sad.

Alonee watched Sereeta walk up to the statue of Harriet Tubman. Sereeta stopped there and tore the pretty paper and ribbons off the box. She bunched them up and put them in a nearby trash can. Then Sereeta opened the box and took a pad of paper from her purse. She wrote something and put it into the open box. She propped the box near the statue pedestal. Then Sereeta walked toward the bike rack, unlocked her bike, and rode toward her grandmother's house.

Alonee went over to the box and knelt down. She read the note.

To somebody who would like this top, size small, take it. It cost twenty-seven dollars on sale. I bought it for someone I loved. She didn't want it—or me!

Alonee had tears in her eyes when she got up. She wanted to run after Sereeta and somehow comfort her. But she couldn't. Sereeta had to heal in her own way.

As Alonee was walking away from the box, two girls ran up to it.

"Tarin, look!" one of them cried. "Is that an awesome top!"

"Did you read the note? That's so sad," the other girl remarked.

"Tarin!" the first girl exclaimed, "It's my size! Oh my gosh! I can't believe this. It's my size and my colors! Should I take it? It's so pretty. Oh, I love it!"

"Yeah, Delilah, take it. It was meant for you," Tarin urged her.

Delilah picked up the top and held it to herself. "Oh Tarin, I thought this was gonna be a bad day. I flunked a chem quiz this morning. And Tommy Fricke didn't even look at me in lab. But look at this beautiful top and it's free! You sure you don't want it, Tarin?"

"I'm a large girl," Tarin laughed.

Alonee returned to her father's car, climbing in quickly beside him. He looked at her. "You're crying, baby. What's going down?" he asked.

Alonee told her father what Sereeta had done with her mother's gift. "A girl came right away and got it. She was so happy," Alonee explained. "Oh Daddy, isn't there something we can do? Should we try to find out why Sereeta's mother didn't come? If she was really sick, that might make Sereeta feel better."

"No baby, we can't do that," Mr. Lennox said. "She's a sick lady. She does not know what she's doing to herself and Sereeta."

"But Sereeta's mom wasn't too sick to go to her own party Friday night," Alonee argued. "Sereeta's old friend called. She said Mrs. Manley was in the front yard in a beautiful dress."

"Yeah, we got a call from the Thornes Friday night too," Alonee's father added. "The party got out of hand. The neighbors had to call the police. Don't you understand, baby? Livy's a binge drinker. She probably had a hangover the size of Texas even on Sunday."

Alonee fell silent for a while, then spoke. "I hope Sereeta wins that princess thing. I know she said she doesn't want it. But I know it would give her a boost. I'm going to vote for her. She needs something good to happen."

"Yeah, it would show her how much the kids love her," Alonee's father agreed. "Good idea, baby."

"Sereeta is hard to figure sometimes, Daddy," Alonee went on. "She's nice and kind and stuff. But she's, you know, damaged. And I don't know how to really help her."

"You can do your best for her, like Sami Archer did, moving the party over to the grandmother's house" her father suggested. "Your mama said that was just the best medicine for Sereeta in the world. That was a beautiful thing. It took Sereeta's mind off the sad thing that had happened. It showed her her grandmother's love and the love of her friends. That's what she needed right then and there. But you can't fix the girl, Alonee. It's like a broken bone. It's got to heal by itself and slowly. Then it'll be good and strong again. One day Sereeta'll probably make a great mother. I once read an essay by a father who'd grown up without a dad. He was abandoned by his father when he was two. He said that experience didn't cripple him in his own role as a dad. He said because of that he was able to be a really good dad because he knew what he had missed."

When Alonee and her father got home, Oliver's BMW was in the driveway. Oliver was leaning on the fender.

"Hey Alonee! Hey Mr. Lennox!" he called out as they pulled in.

Alonee's father greeted Oliver and then went into the house. Alonee went over to Oliver. Oliver pecked a kiss on her mouth and asked, "How goes it, babe?"

"Okay," she said, "but I'm worried about Sereeta. She feels so hurt that her mom didn't come to that party we all planned. She's hurting really bad. You know what, Oliver? You need to vote for Sereeta for the princess thing. I know she said she didn't want it. But it would cheer her up anyway. We've got to do something to make her feel better."

"But she said if they picked her she'd decline it, Alonee," Oliver protested. "I think that kind of publicity on her right now would be painful. Sereeta isn't a show-off even when she's happy. And when she's sad . . ."

"Oliver," Alonee told him, "I know what you're saying. But if she knew how much all the kids loved her, maybe, you know, it would lift her up."

"She knows right now that she's got a lot of good friends, Alonee," Oliver said. "She's got a grandma who loves her. But . . . you know, she doesn't have a mom."

"We can't do anything about that, Oliver, but—"

"Alonee," Oliver cut in. "Listen to me. The girl has a big hole in her heart where her mom should be. We can't fill it with a princess crown. It'd be like if somebody said to me, 'Hey, Alonee doesn't love you. That's okay. You've just been elected Mr. Cheeseburger of the Year. Here's your mustard-colored crown.'"

"So," Alonee said, "we just stand by and do nothing, right?"

"No," Oliver countered. "We got her back. When she needs a friend, it's us. Sometimes family falls short. That's what friends are for. Shoulders to cry on. Stand by her when she's hurting. But she has to go through some of the darkness alone. We all do." Oliver reached out and took Alonee's chin between his fingers. "But at the end of that long, dark tunnel there's light. That's the love of our friends."

CHAPTER TEN

The next morning, as Oliver and Alonee walked to their first classes, Everette Keenan and several friends hurried by. They were talking about the latest polls— which girl was gaining, which was going down.

"I got Neely on top now," one boy said breathlessly.

"No way!" Everette protested. "My guys are still going for Sereeta."

Oliver looked toward the boys. "They're just polling guys, you know. As if the girls didn't have a vote!"

"Next thing you know they'll be taking bets," Alonee remarked. "Maybe that's already happened."

"Once this is over," Oliver figured, "Ms. Amsterdam will probably think of something worse. Could three-legged races be just around the corner? Hula hoop competitions? I'm with Mr. Pippin. This woman has got to be stopped. Or else before we know it we'll be bobbing for apples."

That same morning, as Jasmine Benson ate breakfast, she got her last, desperate idea to turn the tide in her favor. She had heard that she was trailing in the number three spot and continuing to lose ground. She became more frantic as the vote neared. There were just two more days until the juniors would cast their ballots. Everything she had tried to do to give herself an edge had failed. The buzz around school was that Neely Pelham would probably win even though her camp used illegal tactics, passing her photos around. Too many guys saw the stunning pictures. They were sold on Neely now.

"Jasmine," her mother said at the breakfast table, "you don't look well this morning. Is something wrong? You've been too stressed out over that contest at school. Get serious, girl. It's not that important. It's not like getting good grades and getting into a fine college. Jasmine, you even got dark circles under your eyes. Have you been getting enough sleep?"

"I'm okay, Mom," Jasmine replied. Earlier she had stood before the mirror and applied dark shadow under her eyes. She didn't apply her usual bright red lip gloss. She used a pale shade. She made up her beautiful face in a different way.

After her mother dropped her off at Tubman High, Jasmine walked slowly into a large group of students. She knew most of them. "How's it going, Jasmine?" Carissa Polson asked. "The vote's coming up quick now."

"I don't really care anymore," Jasmine answered in a weary voice. "It doesn't matter to me now. I'm just hoping I get to do my senior year here at Tubman or *anywhere*."

"What are you talking about, Jasmine," Alonee asked. "You're doing good in all your classes."

"Oh, it's not that," Jasmine replied, "it's just . . . oh, I'd rather not talk about it."

"What's the matter, Jasmine?" Destini asked. "Are you okay? You don't look so good. Are you sick or something?" Destini had no use for Jasmine because of what she had done. Still, if she was really sick . . .

"My mother took me to the doctor," Jasmine explained, "'cause of this stuff that's been happening to me. They took tests, but it doesn't look good."

Alonee approached Jasmine. "What seems to be wrong, Jasmine?" she asked. By now a couple of dozen students were standing around, listening to the conversation. Almost all of them looked concerned. It seemed as if Jasmine had a serious illness. That was something that happened to older people—to grandparents. When it happened to someone their age—only sixteen years old—it was startling and tragic. It made everybody feel vulnerable.

"I just feel so tired. And I'm losing weight," Jasmine continued. "And there are other things. It's just too depressing to talk about." Her eyes seemed to moisten, and she hurried away.

Alonee looked at Oliver. "Wow, that's outta nowhere. Jasmine sick? I wonder what could be the matter with her."

"Sounds grim," Carissa added. "She's not my best friend or anything. But that's scary, huh?"

Word of Jasmine's illness spread throughout Tubman High quickly. She was not necessarily well liked, but she was well-known. The idea that Jasmine had some mysterious and perhaps serious malady struck everyone with concern. Most of the students at Tubman had known Jasmine since elementary school and, for better or worse, she was one of them.

At lunchtime, Jasmine went off to a secluded place under some pepper trees to eat. When she finished her yogurt, she lay on the grass and stared up at the sky. She thought of sad things, like her grandmother being so lonely in the nursing home. Jasmine never wanted to visit her. But still she felt sad for her grandmother. The old lady had been a nice grandma before she got sick. Just thinking of sad things made Jasmine cry. And she wanted to cry.

Someone who was suddenly very sick ought to cry, oughtn't they?

"Jasmine," a familiar voice came to her as she lay on the grass.

Even without turning her head, Jasmine knew who it was. "Go away, Marko," she commanded.

He came closer. He sat down on the grass near her. "I heard kids sayin' you were sick. What's that all about?" he asked. "What's wrong with you, girl?"

"Just leave me in peace. You'll know when it happens," Jasmine snarled.

"When what happens?" Marko said in a strangely broken voice. "What are you sayin' girl?" He put his face in his hands and sat there. Then he spoke to her. "Jasmine, talk to me. I still love you. I never stopped loving you. You just made me so mad . . . I didn't want to hang with Neely. My heart's been achin' for you, girl. Jasmine, you can't be gettin' sick and, you know, leavin' me. You can't be. Y'hear what I'm sayin'?"

"Nothing matters anymore," Jasmine responded. "The kids don't have to vote for me for princess. I probably couldn't even do the job. But I'd try. I guess it'd be good if I won. Even if I'm sick, I'd do my best . . . "Jasmine turned and looked at Marko. "How could you love me, fool? You treated me like dirt."

"I do love you, baby . . . I do. You gotta get well," Marko begged.

Oliver Randall heard Jasmine crying. He saw Marko sitting beside her with a terrible look on his face. He came over to them and asked, "What's this all about?"

"She's sick. She's really sick," Marko explained.

"Jasmine," Oliver said, "you seemed fine yesterday in Mr. Pippin's class."

"It's been coming on for a long time," Jasmine answered. "I ignored the symptoms.

173

THE FAIREST

Just tell the other girls I wish them luck. If anybody votes for me, well, that's okay. I guess if my time is coming, at least I'd go happy, you know . . . To leave this world knowing all the juniors really liked me, I guess I could go with a smile on my face."

Oliver left the couple to find Alonee. She was talking to some friends at Harriet Tubman's statue.

"Alonee, have you heard about Jasmine?" he asked.

"Yeah . . . it's strange," Alonee said.

"Look," Oliver pointed. "There's Jasmine's mom driving up in the middle of the day. I guess Jasmine must be feeling so bad she called her mom to come get her."

As Jasmine's mother crossed the campus, Alonee and Oliver met her. "We're so sorry to hear that Jasmine is sick, Mrs. Benson," Alonee told her.

"Sick?" Mrs. Benson asked. "Did she get sick here at school? She seemed okay this morning, though she did look a little under the weather. Dark circles under her eyes."

Alonee and Oliver looked at one another. Oliver thought the unthinkable first. Was it possible? Surely it couldn't be. Could Jasmine have pretended to be sick in a last-ditch effort to gain sympathy and perhaps become Princess of the Fair that way? "No," Oliver thought, "not even Jasmine would do such a thing . . . or *would she*?"

"Mrs. Benson," Alonee explained, "Jasmine said you took her to the doctor. They took tests, and it wasn't looking good."

"Took her to the doctor?" Mrs. Benson snapped. "What's going on here? I found the English report she was supposed to turn in today laying on her bed. I brought it here to school. I had to take time off from work. Where is she?"

Oliver and Alonee led Mrs. Benson to the spot under the pepper trees where Oliver had last seen her. As they approached, Jasmine was in Marko's arms. He was tenderly stroking her back.

"Look," Mrs. Benson declared with disgust. "She's with that fool again, the one who put the smelly chicken in her locker. That girl is going to be the death of me yet. Marko Lane turned on her like a snake. And now she's all kissy face with him."

Mrs. Benson stomped up and yelled, "Marko Lane, you get away from my daughter. You didn't treat her right and you know it!"

"Mrs. Benson," Marko stammered. "She's sick . . ."

"Jasmine Benson," her mother yelled. "I brought you the English report you need for that Mr. Pipper."

"Mr. Pippin," Jasmine said in a small voice.

"I don't care if his name's Peter Piper," Mrs. Benson said, throwing down the report. "Now . . . what's this about you being sick, girl? What kind of lies are you telling now? You know what, Jasmine? That pretty little nose of yours is going to grow long as a carrot one of these days."

Jasmine took the English report and began to cry. "I'm s-sorry, Mommy," she wailed, scrambling up the hill and fleeing.

"She's so anxious to win that princess contest. She must've thought pretending she was sick would get kids to vote for her out of pity," Mrs. Benson figured, muttering to herself. "I heard her last night on her phone saying that dying people get a lot of sympathy. I didn't pay any attention to what she was saying then. But I guess that's what happened." Mrs. Benson had fire in her eyes. "That girl is *so* grounded. She is so grounded she'll forget what the world looks like outside of school and her own bedroom!"

After Mrs. Benson left, Marko looked stunned. "She ain't dying then?" he asked. A big smile broke on his face. "That's great. That's really great! We're friends again. She's my chick again. She's one crazy chick, but she's mine!"

Oliver shook his head and smiled. "I hope I never in my life want anything so bad as Jasmine wants that tiara. If I do, I think I'll stick my head in a bucket of ice water until I come to my senses."

The following day, all the juniors at Tubman High were issued ballots to vote for Princess of the Fair. They were to write in the name of any junior girl they wanted. Ms. Amsterdam and several other teachers were going to tally the ballots. They would announce the winner on Thursday afternoon.

At the end of classes on Thursday, a large crowd of juniors gathered in front of the statue of Harriet Tubman. Ms. Amsterdam took the microphone in hand and, beaming widely, made the announcement. "It gives me great pleasure to announce the name of the girl who has been chosen by her peers to be Princess of the Fair. She is a girl of great beauty, like all our junior girls. More importantly she has the qualities of compassion and kindness that are hallmarks of our beloved school namesake,

Harriet Tubman. So without further ado, I give you our princess . . . Samantha 'Sami' Gabriella Archer."

The crowd of juniors erupted in wild applause. They stamped their feet and yelled, "Sam-i! Sam-i!" Most of them had been personally touched by her kindness. Many of the kids were crying with joy. Alonee saw Sereeta Prince hugging Sami. She was only the first of many.

Oliver put his arm around Alonee's shoulders and led her to the foot of statue. He told her, "When Harriet Tubman was dying, she said, 'I can hear the angels singing.' I think Harriet is singing with them now and smiling with pride at what we did today."

The juniors of Harriet Tubman High School had made the fairest choice.